Trouble at Moosehead Lake

**Other Apple Paperbacks
you will enjoy:**

Dirty Socks Don't Win Games
by Dean Marney

The Slime That Ate Crestview
by Jahnna N. Malcolm

Two-Minute Mysteries
by Donald J. Sobol

Welcome to Dead House
by R.L. Stine

The Football Wars
by Scott Eller

Snow Treasure
by Marie McSwigan

Trouble at Moosehead Lake

James and Lois Cowan

AN
APPLE
PAPERBACK

SCHOLASTIC INC.
New York Toronto London Auckland Sydney

DISCLAIMER

Emergency Rescue! stories are fiction. They are meant to encourage young readers to 1) recognize emergencies and 2) seek professional help. The information in the five stories in this book must *not* substitute for medical advice and certified rescue training.

ISBN 0-590-46018-8

12 11 10 9 8 7 6 5 4 3 2 1   3 4 5 6 7 8/9

Printed in the U.S.A.   40

First Scholastic printing, May 1993

Acknowledgments

Our thanks to the following people and dogs for their time, professional guidance, encouragement, and licks: Harry Gray and the dogs of the Perry Green Chinook Kennels; Jim Morrissey, EMT-Paramedic, Vice President, Wilderness Medical Associates; Joseph Walker, Chlorine Institute; David Nazaroff, Winter Mountaineering and Dog Sledding Courses Director, Hurricane Island Outward Bound School; Stanley Quinn, Otis Elevator Company; the students of the North School, Rockland, Maine; Jessie the chinook; A. Frankel, MD, FACEP; Chemical Manufacturers Association; Jean Weber, Massachusetts Society for the Prevention of Cruelty to Animals; Stephen Moore, MD, FACEP; Gareth S. Anderson, Safety Officer, Maine Warden Service, Department of Inland Fisheries and Wildlife; Bonnie F. Staskowski, RN, BS, MBA; Warren D. Holmes, Lecturer, Royal Canadian Police Academy and Instructor, FBI Academy; and Rick Petrie, EMT-Paramedic, Life Safety Consultants of New England.

Dedicated to our real-life Matt,
finer than fiction.

Contents

Decoder Guide

Ten-01	unable to copy	**Ten-32**	person with weapon
Ten-02	receiving well	**Ten-36**	What time is it?
Ten-03	go ahead	**Ten-55**	vehicle accident
Ten-04	OK	**Ten-56**	send a wrecker
Ten-06	I'm busy	**Ten-60**	lost person
Ten-07	out of service	**Ten-61**	hunting accident
Ten-08	I'm available	**Ten-62**	drowning
Ten-09	repeat, please	**Ten-65**	boating accident
Ten-10	out of vehicle	**Ten-66**	snowmobile accident
Ten-13	weather		
Ten-19	go to station	**Ten-71**	bomb threat
Ten-20	give your location	**Ten-72**	fire alarm
Ten-21	call by telephone	**Ten-79**	plane crash
		Ten-81	smoke
Ten-23	stand by	**Ten-91**	call your home

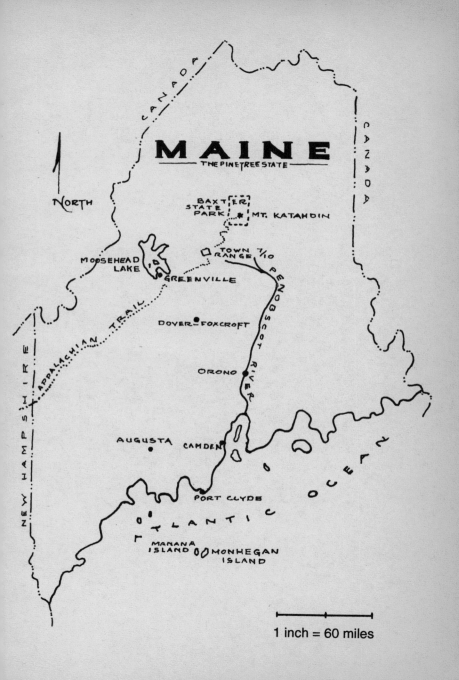

1
Shock

If Moosehead Lake is shaped like a moose's head, then Greenville is its Adam's apple.

The town of Greenville, Maine, hosts the New England Championship Dog Sled Races. Davey, his dad, and stepmom were daytripping north to attend this annual event.

Davey's cousin Matt Rich was going along.

The cousins were pumped.

"Come on, Matt, move it!" Davey Mountain yelled through the cracked-open backseat window. "We're Ten-08. Ready to roll."

"Ten-02, Portable-D." Matt fell in with his cousin's rescue radio-talk. "I'm *en route* to the scene."

Frozen puffs of breath floated behind Matt as he swept down the snow-packed hill.

Everyone in the car held their breath as they watched him weave through the stand of larch trees.

Two years ago, Matt had zigged around these same evergreens when he should have zagged. His knee ended up pierced by a sharp branch.

Davey remembered the day of the accident. He had been the one who called 9-1-1.

It seemed like forever until the ambulance arrived.

Meanwhile, Matt suffered in silence, unable to muster up the courage to look at his damaged knee.

Legs just weren't supposed to be like that, skin and flesh laid open, bits of bark stuck to the wet edges.

It didn't even bleed.

Matt knew, if he looked, he'd see the bones of his knee joint.

But he couldn't stand to *not* look, either.

Tears had run dirty rivers down his cheeks by the time emergency medical technicians and an ambulance arrived.

Now, two years later, something bad — Matt's injured patella bone — had resulted in something good. The boys were intrigued by the crew of EMTs and their gear. And with Puckerbrush Emergency Rescue Squad — the regional fire, medical, access, remote, and harbor rescue teams headquartered in Camden, Maine.

Matt and Davey began to hang around the Puckerbrush Rescue Station like devoted dalmation pups.

They lapped up emergency information and sniffed out survival adventures.

Some of their friends followed the New England Patriots. Others liked rock music. Matt and Davey loved Puckerbrush Rescue because it meant they were involved, not just watching or listening.

* * *

As Matt careened through the snow-blanketed flower bed, Mrs. Mountain opened the car door.

Behind the wheel, Davey's dad checked his watch. He always said Matt was like an English muffin. Seems like it'll never toast, then, *boing*! Up it pops, right on time.

Matt dove into the backseat across his cousin's lap and the sports pages.

Mr. Mountain twisted around to face his nephew. "On the button, Matt."

"Hey, Portable 68," Matt answered, using his uncle's rescue code name.

Davey smoothed the NBA standings.

Matt's winter-tanned face tilted toward Davey's stepmom in the front seat. "Hi, Portable-40." His grin was loaded with braces.

Through a flirt of snow, Mr. Mountain backed out. He aimed the red car, with its emergency light mounted on the dash, north toward the sled races at Moosehead Lake.

As he drove, the Saab's dashboard flasher and special license plate — with an FF after the number — told everyone that Mr. Mountain was a firefighter.

He adjusted the beeper on his hip. When there was a fire, that small box would let loose with a loud tone. Then, with the red emergency light on his car twirling, Mr. Mountain would be off to the station.

But today was a perfect day for a winter outing. With his beeper in a comfortable position, Mr. Mountain leaned back and patted his wife's hand.

Portable-40, Jill Mountain, was also on call with Puckerbrush Rescue. As an emergency medical technician, she helped her sick or injured Camden neighbors. "Puckerbrush Rescue to Portable-40," the big black EMT radio on her hip would burp, "Portable-40. . . . Ten-19 to the station."

"Portable-40 to Puckerbrush," she would answer. "I'll be Ten-08." And she would be off on a run — another medical mission.

Between the fire and EMT radios and the scanner monitoring ten other channels, the Mountain household's radio traffic sounded at times like an airport control tower.

"Remember last year," Davey said to Matt as he folded the sports section and opened a map of Maine, "when that lead sled wiped out at the finish?"

"Right. The chinook team. Think they'll run this year? I hope so."

Matt loved to watch the chinooks. This unusual breed of handsome dogs had been bred to work Ant-

4

arctic expeditions and haul freight during Alaska's gold rush days. When gold had run out and exploration slowed, the breed had almost vanished.

Now dog sled racing was popular in northern New England. And chinooks were making a comeback. Muscular, hardy, and swift, they were winning races.

And a place in the hearts of dog mushers and kids.

Thinking about the chinooks, Matt fell silent. The memory of Queen, a husky-type he raised from a puppy, flooded over him. Queen had been waiting for Matt's school bus when she was run down.

He felt himself choking up. Still.

Matt's mom, Mr. Mountain's sister, had said he could get a new pup. But he never did. Maybe he was afraid to love a new dog. What if something happened to it, too?

* * *

Two hours northwest of Camden, the road began to rise and fall through the Western Foothills.

The land roughened. Frozen ponds dotted the landscape. Here and there, farms seemed to be competing with rocky outcrops.

Then the woods overwhelmed all but streams crusted with ice. Spruce and pine towered near the road. Beyond was Maine's highest peak, snowy Katahdin.

Matt rubbed a peephole in the fog on his window. In a blink, the highway would cross the Appalachian Trail. Someday, Matt promised himself, he'd hike that route from Maine to Georgia. Once his limp was better. And he'd drag Davey along.

As Matt massaged his knee, the road flattened.

"See any place to stop for lunch, Jill?" Mr. Mountain asked his wife.

In the backseat, the boys' stomachs leapt to attention. Davey slipped a Toblerone chocolate bar back into his jacket pocket.

On the highway, the sun glistened off a patch of glare ice.

Matt straightened. He pointed off the road. "Whoa! Up ahead. Is that an overturned truck — a Ten-55 — in the ditch?"

As Mr. Mountain braked, Mrs. Mountain pulled rubber gloves from the glove compartment, in case someone was injured.

Davey put on his old Red Sox cap and bent over, lacing up his Bean boots.

The red Saab inched to a stop on the ice.

Matt hopped out and stood still, in an out-of-the-way spot, leaning against the Saab's black convertible top.

Matt's throat felt like he'd swallowed a glob of peanut butter. *Who's in the truck? Or what? What's the deal? Is the scene safe?* He waited for instructions.

Then he spotted the man, sprawled in snow beside the truck's cab. Not moving.

Is he . . . dead?

His aunt was at the patient's head. "Are you okay?" Mrs. Mountain checked for consciousness. "Can you hear me?" Louder.

The wheels of the flipped pickup spun in the winter air.

A dog whined.

Now Portable-40 was checking to see if the motionless man was breathing.

For Matt, not knowing was worse than anything.

He heard it again. The whine. Maybe from inside the truck?

By the road, Mr. Mountain had grabbed the medical jump kit from the little convertible.

"Any injuries?" Davey asked as he climbed out.

"One," said his father over his shoulder as he headed for his wife holding out a pocket mask.

Mrs. Mountain placed its inflated plastic edges over the man's mouth and nose. As she sealed the mask completely tight, a dog bellied out from the upside-down cab behind her.

Like a ghost.

Only Matt saw.

Matt's aunt leaned forward to blow through the mouthpiece of the pocket mask. Her breath traveled from the man's mouth and nose, through his throat, to balloon his lungs.

The man's chest rose, then fell.

Whew, thought Matt. *His airway's open.*

Matt's gaze shifted to the big dog, struggling to

make sense of the accident scene. The dog's disorientation wouldn't last. Not with the man lying there in the snow — maybe dead.

The dog shook its ears, clearing cobwebs, then zeroed in on the strange woman bent over its master.

The dog's head lowered, eyes no longer spacey.

Matt tensed.

The dog clutched. Neck hairs stood on end.

"Aunt Ji — " Before Matt could get it out, the dog closed the distance between itself and Matt's aunt.

Mrs. Mountain paused. The vanilla-colored dog was checking her out. Without taking its eyes off her, it licked the man's cheek.

Matt's aunt puffed in another one-second breath, then positioned her fingers on the man's neck below the corner of his mouth.

"Pulse," Matt reasoned aloud. His aunt was feeling for the carotid, the pulse closest to the heart and the last to go when the heart no longer pumps.

The dog continued working on the man's face.

Hopefully one of their treatments will work, thought Matt.

* * *

Help was as close as dialing 9-1-1.

Davey nudged Matt and pointed at a vacant gas station down the road. There was a telephone booth out front.

The boys conferred. Was the man alive? Was his

8

heart beating? Mrs. Mountain's fingers were still checking out the carotid pulse for a full fifteen seconds to see.

"When Mom reports on breath and pulse," Davey told Matt, "you run to the phone to activate the emergency medical services system. I'll stay here, wait for EMS, and monitor the scene."

"Ten-04," agreed Matt.

Both boys were up, charged with adrenaline. But they moved with purpose. Cool on the outside. They were part of the rescue team.

"Tell 9-1-1," Mrs. Mountain directed as she leaned over to rescue-breathe, "one adult male patient. No breath. Has pulse."

The dog, still close to its master, licked Mrs. Mountain's wrist, letting its tongue linger against her skin. Brown eyes looked up into her green ones.

She delivered her unused oxygen to the man. "I'm trying," she told the dog between breaths.

Matt sprinted for the pay phone.

He ripped the receiver off the hook. No coin was needed to activate the EMS system. Matt punched in a nine and two ones. "No breath, has pulse; no breath, has pulse," he repeated to himself. "No breath, has pulse."

After his initial report, Matt answered dispatch's questions. When he was told to stay on the line until the emergency medical services arrived, he blurted, "Okay, but tell EMS to hurry!" Then he kicked himself. *Got to stay calm*, he thought. *Don't lose it again.*

Matt squinted back down the road and waited. And waited. It was like a full count, bases loaded, and two outs in the ninth. . . . *Where's that pitch?*

Down the road, Davey kept watch. As soon as he saw the flashing red lights, he raised his arm high and directed the arriving ambulance.

* * *

Five miles up the Greenville road, Phillip Chien — unaware of the accident — prepared for Chinook Kennel's third try for the championship.

Last year, his dog sled team was in the lead when Tornado, the dog in the left-point position, faltered and fouled the tow line. Nine dogs had come crashing down in a heap of tails and snarls. The sled flipped.

In spite of this mishap, Phillip knew Tornado was a promising rookie. So good that he'd been training the big chinook as a pinch-runner for the lead dog, Jet Stream.

Just in case.

In fact, Phillip was just realizing that his father and Jet Stream should be back from the vet by now.

As Phillip slipped the harness over Tornado's head, the back half of her body wagged her tail. The dog musher put pressure on the nylon lead, commanding "Haw." The bulk of Tornado's chinook head turned left. Her feet followed. "Gee," ordered Phillip, pronouncing the g hard, as in goose. Tornado's square snout aimed over to the right, toward a pack of chinooks noodling around.

" 'Nado's wired, aye, Phil?" asked his wife, Marie, as she muscled a fifty-pound feed bag off the back of the truck.

"The rest of the team, too," answered Phillip, gesturing at the crowd of chinooks.

There they were, off to the side of the truck, a flurry of fidgets. Sitting dogs, their tongues dangling, got up, while dogs that had been standing now folded into the snow like collapsing card tables.

Shaking his head at the confusion, Phillip mumbled, "*Plus ça change. . . .*" The more things change, the more they remain the same. Somehow it always ended up with four dogs standing, four sitting, and three on the ground.

Phillip filled the dogs' water bucket from a jerry can on the truck's tailgate.

Behind the water can, in the truck's bed, were two layers of homemade cages. Mobile doggie condos, built into the sides of the truck. The travel home for twelve dogs.

A sled sat on top.

A second sled was on the snow. Nor'easter was nosing every inch of its leather and wood.

The dog's leg lifted.

"Hey!" Phillip yelled.

Nor'easter, his tail between his legs and a coy smile

on his face, traipsed over to the water pail. He sidled up to Tornado, who was drinking.

Two tongues lapped in synch.

Phillip studied his animals. *They'd be champs this year for sure!*

He thought about how much this would mean to his dad. . . .

As a young man, Phillip's father, Shorty, had left his Maine home near the French Canadian border for Alaska. During the Alaskan summers, he fished offshore on commercial trawlers. In the wintertime, he worked as a dog musher.

When Shorty moved back to Maine, he carried a memory of the awesome Pacific Northwest wind, the chinook. And dreams of another chinook, a breed of golden sled dogs that could run like that fierce wind.

Now Chinook Kennel — Shorty, Phillip, Marie, and a few dozen dogs — was popularizing the breed. Larger and faster than the blue-eyed Alaskan husky and with flopping ears, chinooks loved three things.

Kids.

Sleds.

And racing.

Tornado sat at Phillip's feet. As she looked up at him, water dripped from her jowls onto his boots.

"I know," he ruffled her ears, "you're wanting to lead, *ma chérie.* But calm down. Jetty'll be here in a flash."

Phillip glanced toward the parking area.

Where were those two?

*   *   *

The victim started breathing just as the EMTs were Ten-10, at the scene.

They worked carefully and efficiently. To avoid the possibility of further injury to his spine, the man was packaged — strapped to a flat board so his back couldn't curve or bend. If his spine was damaged, and if there was movement, he could end up paralyzed.

EMTs, the chinook right beside them, lifted the stretcher.

On his way to the ambulance, the man opened his eyes. "*Où est* Jet Stream? Where's my dog Jetter? Is she okay?"

"It's all right," said an EMT as he stepped up into the rig. "Your dog's standing right here, sir. She's fine. Just try to relax."

The ambulance doors closed. The dog stood next to Matt and Davey. She looked at the ambulance. Then up at the boys.

"It's okay, girl." Matt patted the dog's head.

Flashing blue lights caught Mr. Mountain's attention. "Davey, watch the dog." A police cruiser pulled over. "I'll fill the police in while Mom finishes up. And then" — Davey's father ruffled Matt's yellow hair — "we'll head for the races."

As Mr. Mountain turned away, the dog moaned.

13

Worried sick about its master, thought Matt.

Davey looked down. "Matt, this dog looks weird. We got a situation here."

Jet Stream's head drooped.

She whined, weakly, then sat. Heavily.

Matt lifted the chinook's muzzle, examined her face. The dog's pupils rolled up into her head. With its wide chin poised in the palm of Matt's hand, the dog looked as if she had up and died.

"Whoa, Portable-D, we've got our own emergency here." Matt heard himself, swallowed, and looked to his cousin. "Hope you know," he said in a lower voice, "what to do with this mutt here."

The dog's lids fluttered. She crumpled into a heap.

Matt shook the dog. "Jet Stream. Can you hear me? Wake up. Bark!"

Davey stared at the unconscious dog. "We don't know anything about *dog* emergencies, Portable-M."

"Let's use common sense." If only those eyes would close, instead of showing a slit of white. The dog looked worse than gone. "Seems like what works for people," Matt figured, "would work for dogs. More or less. First, is the scene safe?"

Davey looked around for his parents. "Good question. The dog's friendly. And unconscious."

Matt thought about his aunt Jill with the unconscious man. He pulled the dog's head back so its tongue wouldn't be in the way of breathing. "I'd better check for breath." He placed his cheek near the dog's nose, his hand on its chest.

In a few seconds he looked up at his cousin. "No."

"No breath? Are you serious?"

Matt shook his head. "We're in deep sneakers here. Hmm. Rescue breathing — on a dog? We've got to give it a try, Portable-D."

Holding the brown muzzle, Matt kept the dog's head straight out like Aunt Jill had done with the man.

"Airway established," said Davey. "Hopefully."

"Right." Matt gestured with his head toward Davey. "Now you give a breath."

"*Me!* Why me? I don't even know this dog!"

"Come *on*. If her brain doesn't get oxygen, she's gonna die." He took in Davey's expression. "Awwwright. If you won't, I will. Can you at least wipe the slobber off her mouth?"

"Mouth?" asked Davey. "Your mouth'll *never* cover this dog's." He paused. "Maybe I can seal it with my hands and then you breathe into her nose. . . . Wait, I've got an idea."

Davey unknotted the bandanna around his neck.

He centered the rolled cloth on top of Jet Stream's muzzle.

Then he passed the ends under the dog's chin and back up the opposite side.

A square knot tied Jetty's mouth shut. No need to

15

worry about bites. And a corner of the bandanna could cover the dog's nose so Matt wouldn't have to come in direct contact with it. Jet Stream prepped for mouth-to-nose breathing. Human-to-dog.

Davey held the dog's head up in a sniffing position. "Go for it, Portable-M," he prodded. "Start rescue breathing."

The boys shared a plan. They were a team.

Matt threw his head back and filled his lungs with air. He covered the dog's nose with his mouth. As he puffed through the bandanna into her snout, his right hand was on Jet Stream's ribs. He could feel her heart beating.

Jet Stream's ribs didn't rise. Something had stopped Matt's breath from entering her lungs.

Matt spit into the snow. "Yeeuck-oh!"

Maybe Jetty's tongue was blocking her throat. Davey again straightened the chinook's head. "I've repositioned the airway. Try again," he urged Matt.

Maybe they'd get lucky. If the dog's brain cells didn't get oxygen, the brain would stop telling the rest of the body to work.

Sweat ran down Matt's sides under his shirt and parka.

"Come on," he pleaded. He took another gulp of air.

He placed his mouth over the dog's nose. Exhaled.

This time Matt felt and saw his hand on the rib cage lift, then drop.

16

Matt's air had gone in, and back out.

The boys knew they had an airway.

Jet Stream's blood was picking up Matt's oxygen. From the lungs, through the heart, to the brain. The dog's brain had oxygen — Matt's oxygen. Jetty's brain could again send messages to other body parts. Hang in there, stomach. Keep pumping, heart.

Even if she were not breathing.

Three more times Matt exhaled into the dog's nose. After each breath, he and Davey watched her ribs, hoping they'd lift on their own.

They didn't.

Please rise, Matt said to himself. He imagined his own dog, Queen, lying dead beside the road.

Please.

* * *

Nothing.

Until after the fourth try. Slight movement.

Jetty had taken a breath! A shallow one.

Then another. Deeper.

Her eyes opened. She gazed at Matt. She blinked. Twice. Snorted.

"She's regained consciousness, Matt," said Davey just as his father walked up to them. "Breathing on her own!"

* * *

"ATTENTION MUSHERS. FIVE MINUTES TO THE START OF THE NEW ENGLAND CHAMPIONSHIP DOG SLED RACES. A-DIVISION TEAMS GO TO

17

YOUR ASSIGNED STATIONS." The tangle of men, women, dogs, and sleds erupted like popcorn in a hot skillet. "FIVE MINUTES TO THE START. *FIVE MINUTES.*"

Barks, howls, and growls rose from the Chinook Kennel staging area. Four pairs of dogs had been hitched to the sled. The chinooks were slamming at their harnesses, raring to go.

Jet Stream's place at the lead stood empty.

"Where *are* they?" Phillip didn't know whether to be angry or worried. "I knew," he muttered into his beard, "I shouldn't have let the two of 'em drive up by themselves."

One last time he peered back down the highway in the direction of Dover-Foxcroft, the nearest town. "*Eh bien,* 'Nado," he shrugged, "it looks like you're it. Think you can handle it?"

Tornado leapt up, tugging at her tether. Her body language said: Can I ever! That little acccident last year . . . that was just a careless mistake. Oh, Jet Stream's fast. She's won a lot of ribbons for us. But *I've* been training for this all year. I am ready. Lead? You bet!

* * *

Back at the scene of the Ten-55, the ambulance — a mobile emergency department — idled.

Inside, Shorty Chien was checked from head to belly to toe, inside and out. Notes were taken. Bumps, bruises, cuts, and broken bones were treated. A tall

18

green cylinder supplied him with oxygen. The workings of his heart bounced across a monitor screen. The hospital was radioed. Shorty's condition was relayed, along with his ETA. In twenty minutes, Shorty would be wheeled into the Dover-Foxcroft Hospital.

The back door of the rig opened. Mrs. Mountain got out.

"Let's rock and roll," the crew chief called over his shoulder as he grabbed the door to close it. "Thanks again, Jill." He looked down at Mrs. Mountain. "Shorty's stewin' 'bout his dog. Think I could twist your tail to take the mutt over to Moosehead for him?"

* * *

In the backseat, Jet Stream snoozed across the boys' laps. Davey and Matt marveled as her ribs rose and fell, up and down, fifteen times a minute. In their medical opinion, the chinook was resting comfortably. Up and down, in and out. The boys couldn't believe it.

As the red Saab crossed the Greenville town line, Jet Stream's front legs started twitching. Her ears radared. She pulled herself up to a seated, then standing, position to gaze through frost-coated windows.

Matt and Davey scrunched to avoid the effects of Jetty's four paws and her hundred pounds of gristle and fur.

A tail-whop caught Davey right across the mouth.

As the car pulled into a parking space, Matt unbuckled his seat belt. "Ten-32," he sighed. "At last."

They had arrived at the dog sled races.

* * *

The big chinook knew where she was headed as she led Matt and Davey around sleds, teams, and campers. The boys clutched the end of the leash they'd made out of Davey's bandanna, like bulldogs clamped to a mailman's trousers.

The trio skidded to a stop in front of the Chinook Kennel truck. At their feet and paws were two chinooks, their tails over their noses to screen out the freezing air.

The rest of the team was gone, long gone. Somewhere out on the thirty-mile course, Tornado was pointing the way as Phillip pedaled, one foot pushing on the snow and the other riding the sled's runner.

As Marie fussed over Jet Stream, the boys told her what had happened.

Her father-in-law at the hospital? Her hands flew to her cheeks. And Jetty resuscitated? "But why," a wide-eyed Marie wondered, "would Jet Stream stop breathing?"

"A sy-ko-jen-ik reaction." Davey pronounced psychogenic carefully. "The car accident must have scared her so much she lost it. Right, Mom?"

Mrs. Mountain nodded as she considered the MOI — mechanism of injury. "Once Jetty felt your father-in-law was in good hands, Marie, we figure she couldn't keep it together anymore.

"Jet Stream probably fainted from fright. Animals do that." Mrs. Mountain went on to explain that, as Jetty fell, her tongue had landed in a position that closed off her throat.

She couldn't breathe with her airway obstructed.

"Once her airway was clear," Mrs. Mountain continued, "the boys' rescue breathing prodded her lungs into working on their own."

* * *

It was the first week of summer vacation, just four months since Tornado and her team won the New England Championship Dog Sled Races.

Matt and Davey hauled their kayak up onto the dock in front of Davey's house. They peeled off their life jackets.

"I'm dying of thirst," said Matt, raking his blond hair out of his eyes. After a drink, maybe he'd go over to the library and see if they had Gary Paulsen's *Woodsong*. Yeah, then he'd curl up with his favorite author and read about Alaska's Iditarod dog sled race. He was beat.

"Lemonade break," his cousin panted.

Loping through the house toward the kitchen, the boys both looked to the right, into the ceiling-high hall mirror. Matt's reflection loomed behind Davey's. When Matt squared up his shoulders, he was a good five inches taller than his cousin although they were just a few months apart in age.

Matt smiled at the mirror, flashing his braces. He

21

sealed his lips, pushed a blond mop of hair off his high, tanned forehead.

He scanned his cousin's image. Davey's brown eyes, Matt noted, always had a look. Like a hawk on a perch . . . searching off in the distance for something new.

Which is just what he was doing now, as he tugged down his baseball cap and, with both hands, rounded the visor. Davey pointed to the reflection of the hall window opposite the mirror. "Isn't that the Chinook Kennel truck out front?"

As Davey turned and opened the door, a familiar-looking nose pushed its way in.

Jet Stream had come visiting. And Shorty Chien.

"Whoa, girl," laughed Shorty from behind, grabbing at her scruff as she recognized Matt. "You're acting like you died and went to heaven."

"Easy, pooch." Matt knelt on one knee and rubbed Jetty's ears.

This put the chinook into a total tizzy. She planted wet kisses all over his face and neck.

Matt almost missed the whimper sound.

What could that be? he wondered. Davey's bulldog, Bossy, was upstairs in Aunt Jill and Uncle David's office. Anyway, Bossy did rumble-grumble sounds.

Matt re-opened the door and looked out.

"Yip." In a cardboard box on the granite front step, a pint-sized Jet Stream was scratching its way over the edge, to freedom.

"Ah. You found him," said Shorty. "This pup of hers — he's all yours. Jetty wanted to thank you, Matt."

The boy picked up his dog.

The chinook's emery-board puppy tongue tested Matt's cheek.

Matt blew a puff of air at the pup, onto its black nose.

Everyone laughed. Except Jet Stream.

She wagged her tail.

SKILL
Dog Rescue Breathing

WHAT is it? Breathing into a dog's lungs.

WHY do you do it? When a dog doesn't breathe, its brain starts dying. As the brain shuts down, the heart stops pumping. Your breath — even the air you breathe out — contains enough oxygen to prevent this. Matt's oxygen kept Jetty's brain alive while she wasn't breathing.

WHEN do you do it? When a dog isn't breathing. Look, listen, and feel to be sure. Are ribs rising and falling on their own? Can you hear breath sounds? With your cheek, can you feel air from the mouth or nose? If there's no breath, muzzle the dog with cloth or a belt. Only rescue breathe for a dog that you see collapse; Jet Stream had just stopped breathing for only a few seconds when Matt began.

HOW do you do it? By breathing the way you always do. But exhale directly into the dog's nose, not into the air. 1) After muzzling, place dog on its left side. 2) Hold head in a sword swallower's position so air will shoot down into dog's lungs. 3) Place your mouth over nose. Breathe into dog's nostrils. 4) Remove your mouth. If ribs didn't rise, reposition dog's head, as

24

Davey did. 5) Fill your lungs with air. Again place your mouth over dog's nostrils. Blow your breath into dog. 6) After every 20 breaths, stop. Look, listen, and feel. No breath? Repeat 3 through 6. 7) Continue rescue breathing until help arrives. Or the dog begins to breathe, like Jet Stream did.

Is the scene safe?

Don't touch conscious, injured dogs whether or not they are moving. Even your own pet, when hurt, will be scared and dangerous.

Conscious, walking, sleeping dogs are breathing. Dogs who need attention are unconscious — they cannot think or feel. ONLY DO RESCUE BREATHING ON A NON-BREATHING, UNCONSCIOUS DOG.

Never do rescue breathing on an unmuzzled dog.

Do not rescue breathe for a human unless you have been trained.

* * *

To learn more about dog rescue breathing, read *Emergency First Aid for Dogs*, by Consumer Guide Editors, published by Publications Int'l., 1988.

Emergency Rescue! Report

Report number 1	My name MATT RICH

Incident location
DOVER - FOXCROFT ROAD
street
GREENVILLE , MAINE
city/town   state

My address
BAY VIEW STREET
street
CAMDEN , ME. 04843
city/town   state   zip

Was the scene safe? yes ☒ no ☐
Describe the scene.

A TRUCK FLIPPED OVER ON AN ICY ROAD.
THE DRIVER AND HIS DOG WERE INJURED.

First name of victim   Age 73 male   female   **Aid first given by**
SHORTY CHIEN AND JET STREAM 5   ☒   ☒ DOG
- ☒ me (DOG)
- ☐ someone else
- ☒ EMTs (MAN)
- ☐ police
- ☐ firefighters

Transported to DOG TO GREENVILLE
MAN TO DOVER-FOXCROFT HOSPITAL

Describe any transportation or communication problems.
ICY ROADS

Type of illness or injury or accident
- ☒ bone fracture
- ☐ aches and sprains
- ☒ bleeding injury
- ☐ illness
- ☐ fire
- ☒ auto or truck accident
- ☐ water incident
- ☐ HazMat
- ☐ airplane disaster
- ☐ lost person/search and rescue
- ☐ extrication
- ☒ animal incident
- ☐ electrical accident
- ☐ tornado
- ☐ hurricane
- ☐ blizzard
- ☐ other

Who called for help?
- ☒ me
- ☐ a friend
- ☐ family member
- ☐ professional responder
- ☐ neighbor
- ☐ other person

Emergency responders on the scene
- ☒ EMTs
- ☐ firefighters
- ☒ police
- ☐ HazMat
- ☐ emergency department
- ☐ utility crew
- ☐ search and rescue

Describe what happened, and the outcome. Include unusual circumstances. MY AUNT JILL AND SOME EMTs TREATED THE MAN AND THEN TOOK HIM TO A HOSPITAL. WHEN THE DOG FAINTED, DAVEY AND I RESCUED HER BY OPENING HER AIRWAY AND BREATHING FOR HER. THEN SHE STARTED BREATHING ON HER OWN AND WAS OK. AUNT JILL SPOKE WITH MR. CHIEN THE NEXT DAY. HE WAS GETTING BETTER AND WOULD STOP BY TO THANK US WHEN HE GOT OUT OF THE HOSPITAL.   **my signature** Matt Rich

2
Stuck

"Ever see one of these things?" The Augusta chief paused in his firehouse tour.

Mr. Mountain didn't have a clue.

"Elevator key." The chief twirled an aluminum cylinder eight inches long and as thick as a fat fountain pen; a flat bar, like a blunt penknife blade, pivoted at one end. "Solves more problems than you can shake a stick at."

The chief wagged the tool. "You wouldn't believe the fub-ups we see in our tall buildings. 'Specially when kids are involved."

*   *   *

"Check it *out*." Davey Mountain grandstanded into the center of the apartment elevator. He tugged his cap's visor, then reared back on his haunches.

27

His cousin, Matt Rich, slouched against the elevator wall, being cool. For kids from a tiny coastal town with no elevators, this was fun.

The green back-lit buttons blipped up the floors. Two. Three. Four. . . .

Davey, in a squat, tensed.

Five.

He sprang into the air like he was jumping for the tip-off against the Celtics' Robert Parish.

The elevator stopped at the fifth floor, and Davey landed a split-second later. He spread his arms, awaiting applause. "Get it, Matt? If you're airborne as the elevator car brakes, you can't feel it stop."

"Awesome," Matt agreed, as the doors whispered open.

Davey tipped his Red Sox cap to his many fans and brushed off his imaginary uniform. "Yo, Matt, let's get lunch."

As the cousins walked out into the corridor toward Luke Chapel's apartment, Davey trailed his fingertips along the OTIS ELEVATOR COMPANY name recessed into the steel cover plate.

While Davey's dad bunked at the Augusta firehouse, learning about urban rescue, the boys and Davey's stepmom were staying in Luke's apartment.

Luke was a paramedic. He had first met Stacy Rich, Matt's older sister, when he trained her as a WooFeR — a Wilderness First Responder.

Then Mr. and Mrs. Mountain and their niece had

run with Luke on a search and rescue mission. Although their SAR team never found the lost hunter they were looking for, Stacy, her aunt, and her uncle had become fast friends with Luke.

Luke's apartment was the third on the left.

In his kitchen, Mrs. Mountain was pulling one of Luke's bowls from a shelf. "I'm just doing lunch, boys," she told Matt and Davey as they peered into the fridge. "Then I thought you might like to head for the State House to see democracy in action."

"Sure, Mom," said Davey. "Tell you what — Matt and I'll go exploring and we'll be back here" — he consulted his watch — "in ten minutes, Ten-03?"

* * *

Back in the elevator, Davey pressed the lobby button. The car descended.

At the ground level, a man in a striped cowboy shirt with pearl snap buttons stepped in, followed by a very pregnant woman.

The man in the cowboy shirt, a smile pasted on his face, pancaked himself against the back wall.

Neither he nor his smile moved when two elderly ladies, one tall and lean and the other short and soft, got on. Davey thought the shorter one looked a little like his Aunt Rose. She filled him with a curious memory — a blend of hot ironing, floor wax, and baked ham with cloves.

The elevator lifted, stopping at 2. When the doors opened, no one was in sight.

As the steel doors closed, a battered leather brief-case suddenly wedged itself in the crack. With a sigh, the doors re-opened. Holding the briefcase was a pudgy businessman who used his case to move Matt away from the control panel.

The man stabbed 7.

Davey looked at his watch. Five minutes had gone by. He pressed 5.

The elevator stopped at 3.

"Oh. Excuse me, young man, would you please hold the door open for us?"

Matt reached behind the briefcase-armed man and pushed **HOLD**.

A woman with hair like cotton candy pushed her husband's wheelchair through the open door. She looked at the panel. Already lit were 5 and 7. She placed her hand back on the wheelchair handle.

Nine occupants — nine and one-half counting the pregnant lady. To make room, Matt edged toward the corner. Davey stood on tiptoe to look at the elevator license. **Maximum capacity: 10 persons or 1500 pounds.** Close.

"No room for jumping and high-fiving this go-round," Matt said to Davey.

Davey, his elbows out to save himself some space, didn't agree.

Three . . . four. . . . Davey punched himself off the floor and caught air.

With a thump and a lurch, Davey landed while the

elevator was still moving. He'd jumped too soon, he realized as his hip bopped the briefcase on his right.

This caused the pudgy man to squish into the soft, short, old lady.

She bumped her lean friend, looking up at her with an "I'm sorry" look.

Davey pulled his visor low and studied the carpeting. As soon as the door opened, he'd be outta there.

* * *

A couple of miles from Luke's apartment building, inside the Augusta fire station, the chief was replacing the elevator key in Engine Six.

Davey's father stood between the fire truck and a wall of firefighting clothing. On a brass hook in front of him was his mound of turnout gear, topped with his plastic-visored red helmet, D. MOUNTAIN stenciled on its back.

His rubber boots with reinforced steel toes sat underneath.

Drooped around the outside of the boots were yellow bunker pants — quick-hitches.

Between his helmet and boots hung his cumbersome black coat with reflective stripes on back and cuffs.

From a distance, his gear looked like a live, stubby firefighter.

Mr. Mountain knelt down and arranged his red suspenders across his boot tops. When a call came in, he would dive into his boots, pull up his pants, and stretch the suspenders over his shoulders. In one fell swoop.

Cruiser, the firehouse dalmation, had been curled in the corner like a soccer ball. Now she stretched, and eyed Mr. Mountain fussing with his gear. The dog got up and walked over to sniff at this unfamiliar set of turnouts in her fire station.

Mr. Mountain scratched the dog's ears, then stood, pressing the small of his back with his fingertips.

"David." The chief came up behind him. "This here's Art." He gestured toward his dispatcher. "He knows the equipment floor. If you've got questions, ask Art here." He pronounced it, "Aat, heah."

The grizzled dispatcher lifted a forefinger in greeting without looking up, and continued typing.

At his elbow sat the red emergency phone. Waiting.

*   *   *

The elevator door didn't budge.

"It isn't opening." The taller old lady piped up. "It's *a-at* five." She looked at the **DOOR OPEN** button. She thumbed it. She touched the fifth floor button.

"Here." The pudgy businessman shouldered his body through the car, wedging the tall lady into the corner. "Let me do it." He threw her a what-a-wing-nut! expression and pushed the same buttons she had. He punched the sixth, then the fourth floor buttons with the heel of his hand.

32

Nothing.

The elevator was stuck.

Suspended inside its hoistway.

Somewhere.

Holding nine souls hostage. Davey took stock of the situation. Two elderly ladies, now silent; the pregnant woman looming behind the fireplug-shaped businessman; himself and Matt; the woman with the cotton-candy hair, holding the wheelchair handles in a viselike grip; her husband hunched in his seat, eyes on his big knuckles.

And that man in the cowboy shirt with a piano keyboard of smiling white teeth whose expression spelled fear.

Nine tense travellers poised for a vibration. If the elevator moved, would they be better or worse off?

No one knew.

Everyone's worst nightmare.

Davey smelled fear. "This is what you call a situation," he mumbled.

The pudgy man whopped the steel doors with his briefcase, breaking the silence. "Open up! What'd ya' think yur doin'?" The elevator, lacking ears, did not scare. "We're stuck in here." His voice rose. "I need to get out. HELP!"

"What do we do now?" Davey said to no one in particular, wishing he had Camden's fire chief to ask. "I've never heard Chief Oxton on elevator extrication.

33

Rescuing people from cars, houses, sure. Even cows and sheep from burning barns. But elevators?" He shook his head.

"I haven't the faintest, Portable-D. We're in deep sneakers here. But it seems like your basic rescue stuff ought to apply. Let's see — nobody's hurt. No medical emergency." He refused to glance at the bulk of the pregnant woman. "Though," he bent toward his cousin, "I'm worried about that guy over there who was banging on the controls." He pointed with his eyes. "Hmm. He's real quiet now, look. And he's a little green around the gills."

The man sidled into the left front corner. His hand never left the rail.

"What we've got to do, Portable-M," decided Davey, "is to figure a way to activate the 9-1-1 system. And keep everyone calm. Let's angle on over and check out the control panel."

"Doesn't seem as if there's anyone else here who's going to take charge," agreed Matt.

The cousins wormed their way around the wheel-chair.

As Davey passed the cowboy with the synthetic smile, Matt smelled aftershave — Old Spice? His nose picked up sneaker odor. The Aunt Rose-type had on a pair. They might, Davey realized, end up knowing each other better than they'd like.

Matt studied the panel. "Looks like everything's

straightforward here. Seven floors and a basement. Door Open and Door Close buttons."

"It could take days for someone to figure out that we're stuck," exaggerated the tall, thin lady to her friend. As she spoke, her head bobbed and dipped, like a sparrow on guard for cats. "Everyone in the building will think this one's out of order, and they'll just use the other one." She wrung her hands.

This uncomfortable concept became the focus of a group discussion. They shared a problem. It made them feel close.

Yet, as soon as (if!) they got out, the closeness would melt like an ice cube in a heat wave. They would walk away, strangers again.

"Excuse me, ma'am . . . " Matt spoke to the woman with the cotton-candy hairdo who was promising everyone, including her husband who slumped even further into his chair, that there was no problem. No worry at all.

She was repeating herself now for the fourth time, fidgeting with the straps of her straw bag.

Some crew, thought Davey.

". . . could you move your purse, please?" Matt raised his voice over hers.

As she pulled her bag close, a metal panel with a see-through cabinet door was uncovered. Davey looked through its glass. Inside, on a hook, was a phone's handset. A framed card read:

Ah, Davey thought. *That's why there's no emergency button. They've given us a phone!*

Davey put it to his ear, his hand covering the mouthpiece. Then he turned his head and raised his voice. "Can I have all your attention?" The adults looked at him. "I'm Davey Mountain and this is my cousin Matt Rich. We have an emergency phone here. We'll call 9-1-1 now, then we'll tell you what they said."

The pregnant woman's forehead smoothed.

The round businessman took one hand off the rail to muffle a belch.

"Say, kid." The tense cowboy tapped Davey's shoulder. "I've got to have a smoke. If I don't, I'll suffocate in here." His face was a lesson in panic.

Everyone else's expression made clear what they thought of his request.

"Sorry," Davey said.

"Could you maybe," Matt suggested, "take imaginary drags?"

The man's hand unsnapped his pearl pocket button, took out a cigarette. His teeth clamped the filter end. He pretended to light up, sucking in a lungful of smoke. He blew non-smoke into the air above everyone's head.

Meanwhile the man who was shaped like a fireplug

had assumed the gray color of a Megunticook Lake trout.

Davey, beads of perspiration on his forehead, was relieved to hear a phone ringing at the other end.

* * *

BZZZT. BZZZT.

The station's red phone was ringing. It was a dedicated line. When it rang, everyone paid attention. Like the bell at the end of a school day.

At the dispatch console, Art stopped typing.

Throughout the station, all hands paused in their work.

"Augusta Fire Station . . ." Art had licked the end of his pencil and pulled over a pink pad with lines and blanks. Even before he'd finished saying, "How may we help . . . ?" he had filled in the time, date, and run number.

He touched the pencil point to his tongue again as he listened. "You're stuck in an elevator. Okay. What's your name?" Art wrote out D-a-v-i-d. "Can you give me your Ten-40, er . . . your location, please?"

Art continued writing. "The Augusta Arms. Western Avenue, near to McDonald's."

Mr. Mountain looked over Art's shoulder, thinking that something was going on where Jill and the boys were staying. Good thing they're at the State House this afternoon.

"Is anyone hurt?" Art asked Davey. "Good. Now

listen-up while I tell you what we're gonna do. To-gether. Don't hang up. Do you copy me okay?"

* * *

"Matt," whispered Davey, "tell eveyone to quiet down. I've got the fire department on the line, and they're going to get us all out of here. But first I've got to be able to hear instructions."

Matt relayed Davey's message.

The passengers were like skittish horses, shuffling hooves. Everyone turned in Davey's direction. All that had been necessary was a couple of cowboys to round 'em up and get 'em organized.

"I copy, Augusta. Go ahead."

Davey listened, nodding. Then he held the receiver against his chest to report. "Here's the deal. The fire department's rolled a truck. And dispatch tells me the station's about five minutes from here so they should now be . . ." — Davey checked his watch — "they should now be less than two minutes away. Once they get here, they'll get us out."

The boys, with the help of dispatch, had a plan of action. They were doing something and knew it was making a difference. Because of that, even though they were the two youngest people in the elevator, everyone accepted that they were in charge.

"Ahhh, young man." Davey felt a hand on his shoulder. It was the short, soft Aunt Rose in sneaks. "Are we safe here? Is there any way this car could f-f . . . fall?"

38

The cat was out of the bag. Nobody had wanted to bring it up. The bottom line in "Is-the-scene-safe?"questions. Davey knew that he needed to find out. He was afraid that he might not like the answer.

"I'll ask."

* * *

Back at dispatch, Art wrestled with Davey's relayed query.

Next to the dispatch cubicle, Engine Six's bay was empty. With sirens blaring and strobe lights twirling, the fire truck was Ten-08 for the Augusta Arms with the chief, Firefighter Mountain, and two men on board.

The first to respond to emergencies, this attack truck carried the access and extrication equipment needed to get firefighters into, and people out of, difficult spots.

"I want you to know," Art was telling Davey, "and be sure to tell all those others in the elevator with you, that you are in no danger. Riding in an elevator's safer than climbing the stairs. All you have to do is not panic. Help is almost there. The chief'll get you out."

Art paused. Through the phone he heard a loud, high-pitched female voice. Then Davey's calmly worded question about falling.

"Well, no," Art continued. "I can't promise you *that*. I don't really know how those things work. But I'm

sure they have all sorts of safety devices built in.
. . . No, I don't know what they are. What's that? I
can't hear you when you whisper. Uh-huh. I see.
They're stressed out, huh? I agree you need to answer
all questions. Tell you what — how's 'bout I patch
you right through to the chief?"

Fire department ETA was thirty-five seconds from
the apartment building when the radio in the engine's cab squawked: "Augusta headquarters to Engine Six."

"Engine Six, Augusta. Ten-03?"

As the truck came to a stop, the chief threw open
his door and was striding toward the lobby of the
building, now speaking into a two-way radio clipped
to his lapel.

"Chief, the folks in the elevator want assurance
that the darned thing won't fall. I'm patching the kid
through to you. Ten-03?"

"That's an -04, Augusta. . . ."

Back at his dispatch console at the station, Art
turned a dial and flipped a switch.

"We've entered the lobby and are standing right in
front of the two elevator doors," said the chief to
Davey. "Can you hear me?"

The chief's words went from his lapel radio to the
fire station's console and then back out to Davey's
elevator phone — a distance of miles in a split
second.

"That's a Ten-04, Ten-02." The chief's eyebrows

raised. "Loud and clear," Davey added for the benefit of his fellow passengers who were hanging on every word.

At the sound of Davey's voice over the chief's radio, Firefighter Mountain stiffened, then grabbed the chief's arm. "Wait a minute. That's my son! Davey. How the he — "

The chief handed Firefighter Mountain a radio. "Tell him we're going to open an elevator door below them and take a look-see up the hoistway. Once we know where the car is stuck, we'll figure a way to get 'em out."

The chief approached the still-locked door. He held the elevator key he'd shown Mr. Mountain earlier.

The chief flip-flopped the bar from side to side as he examined the elevator door.

His grease-stained finger located a half-inch hole in the top left corner. The elevator key eased in. One inch. Two. *Thunk.* The flattened blade dropped down at a right angle. Now the shaft and the blade were shaped like the letter L.

The chief was on tiptoe. A turn of his ham-hock hand brought the blade against the locking mechanism. The chief teetered. He pushed a bit harder. Metal slid against metal as the doors unlocked. "Got her."

The chief turned to Firefighter Mountain. "Take a hold of my turnout gear in case I lose my balance. Don't want to end up like smashed potatoes." He

41

faced the door and heaved, using the key as a handle.

The doors slid open.

Firefighter Mountain and the chief peered through cables, down the hoistway. In the murk of the sub-basement, they saw the cement pads supporting the base of the shaft.

No elevator cab.

Then they looked up. There it was! Numbers painted on the opposite wall identified locations of the various floors. The car was stuck about halfway between the fourth and fifth.

The chief ordered Firefighter Mountain to climb the stairs to the fourth floor and open the door there.

Then together, they would use the elevator hy-draulics to ease the car down to the fourth-floor level.

Davey's dad climbed the stairs two at a time. On the fourth floor, he used the elevator key to open the doors. Then he could stare up at the bottom of the car, only five feet above. *My son and nephew,* he thought, *are in there.*

Imprisoned in a cage.

He leaned against the wall. His knees felt weak. There was a hole in his stomach big enough to drive the ladder truck through.

* * *

Inside the elevator, the pregnant woman sagged against Matt. "I've got to sit." Her voice was weak. "I think the baby is coming." Her face was pure Mary Poppins. "Will that upset the others?"

He put his arm around her waist and turned to the other passengers. "I'd like to ask you all to sit down." He moved his other hand a little, casually.

"No way," blurped the fireplug. He looked unhappy. Angry. Nauseated.

The pregnant woman plopped down onto the floor.

"But I *am* sitting," said the man in the wheelchair, speaking for the first time. He sounded as if he liked the idea of everyone being down at his level. Or lower.

"Oh, I'm so sorry," fluttered his wife. "Maybe I should continue to stand, to help out a little."

"Sit," her husband told her. She sat. He sat up straight.

The two women friends continued to talk. Everyone ignored them. Except Matt. Who chatted with them both, while patting the thin lady's arm.

They quieted down, and sat.

The man in the cowboy shirt panted, "I have to get out of here!" His clothing was stuck to him in the air-conditioned car.

Claustrophobia. The man couldn't deal with even the thought of a confined space.

"Just sit down and relax. Take a few more puffs," Davey suggested. He gave the man a slap on his back like a catcher with his ace pitcher. Buck up. Keep it together, man.

Davey held the phone under his arm and put his Red Sox cap on backwards. He placed the phone back to his ear.

The chief started to talk.

Davey sat down and listened.

Once everyone was seated, they were calmer.

Except the pregnant woman, who was doubled over, her arms tight around her knees. Davey watched her as he listened to the chief.

"Okay." Davey turned to the group. "Here's the deal. The firefighters say we're stuck between two floors. No, no, it's okay," Davey responded to the wheelchaired man's expression. "It's not a problem. We will be dropp . . . , er, eased down a half floor to the fourth-floor doors. Then, you'll just wheel out. But" — he tried to exude sincerity, convey assurance — "this will require that the electricity be cut off to this car. *NO PROBLEM*, however."

"But," Davey continued, ignoring the newest round of gasps, "the lights *will* go out. . . ."

The shrieks began.

* * *

Back down on the first floor, the chief walked around a corner to the rear of the elevator's hoistway. Using his master key, he unlocked the machine room and stared at the elevator motor and controls.

Then he spoke into his shoulder mike. "Okay, Davey, I'm cutting the power now. Your dad's waiting to open your car when you are level with the fourth floor. Ten-03?"

A quiet voice came through the radio. "Ten-04."

The chief threw the circuit breaker.

In the elevator, the lights went out. There was a new silence as the air-conditioning fan died.

On the first floor, the chief opened a valve and bled out oil to reduce the pressure.

The elevator cab began to move.

Firefighter Mountain, on the fourth floor, watched the car's slow descent. When it was level with him, he radioed the chief. "You got it. Stop. Ten-03?" Then Davey's dad rapped on the still-closed inside doors. "Davey. Matt. I'm right here. Just hold on."

On the other side of the door, the pudgy man barfed all over his briefcase, splashing the short lady's sneakers. "Oh, pugh!" She was displeased. "Yeeuck!"

"No problem, Dad," Davey yelled back, dealing with his own gag reflex. "The scene's under control, Ten-04." He looked at the yucky floor. "Sort of."

* * *

At the same moment Davey's dad pried open the elevator doors, Augusta's EMTs arrived on the scene.

Mr. Mountain bear-hugged his nephew and son. The man in the wheelchair looked at them. "Your boys saved the day," he told Mr. Mountain. "If I ever get stuck again, I hope it's with them. Ho ho." Then he wheeled off, his wife trotting to keep up.

The medics' attention focused on the pregnant lady. She was packaged on a cot, then rolled into the other elevator.

Everyone else went back to their own lives, including Mr. Mountain, Davey, and Matt.

45

As they climbed the stairs to the fifth floor, the boys filled Mr. Mountain in on their experience.

"Sounds like," Mr. Mountain said, "you guys did everything right, even with a baby on the way."

"D'ya think, Uncle David," asked Matt, "if it's a boy, she'll name him Otis?"

"Or Lotus," said Davey as he rang Luke's doorbell, "if he's a girl."

Mrs. Mountain opened the door. At the sight of her husband, she lit up. "Honey! What — " her words were muffled as they hugged, " — are you doing here?"

Mr. Mountain looked over his wife's head and said to the boys, "Guys, go sit and eat. Your lunch's waiting." He gestured toward the dining room table.

Mrs. Mountain took his firefighter's coat. He bent to remove his boots.

Davey stayed put. "But Mom, weren't you worried about us?"

"Well, yes and no. Matt's always right on the button. But you, Davey, it'd take more than your being fifteen minutes late for me to worry."

It had felt like an hour.

With the adults joining in, Matt and Davey relived their escapade as they all wolfed down tuna and cheddar cheese sandwiches.

"So the chief doesn't really understand what happened. He figures the control panel, or a button, got jammed. But that wouldn't just happen," concluded

46

Davey's dad. "Someone'd have to have been jumping around."

"Hey, Mom, Dad." Davey stood up, bolting his last bite. "Aren't we supposed to be at the State House?" He grabbed his Augusta road map and shoved it in his pocket.

Matt zipped his jacket. "I'm ready, Aunt Jill," he said as he extricated a piece of tuna caught in his braces. "Let's rock 'n' roll."

With Matt and Davey in the lead, they left Luke's apartment munching on Fudge-Covered Oreos.

"Hey guys," said Mrs. Mountain, cupping her palm to catch cookie crumbs, "slow down. You're going the wrong way. Elevator's over here." She cocked her head.

"It's okay, Aunt Jill," called Matt as they headed down the corridor. "We need the exercise. We'll use the stairs. See ya' at the bottom."

SKILL
People Control

WHAT is it? Helping others to cope with an emergency.

WHY do you do it? People react to scary situations in different ways. They might seem confused, or panicked. Your goal is to make victims and bystanders feel that the scene is under control and someone is in charge. This relaxes everyone.

WHEN do you do it? In a crisis. Whenever you spot the signs of stress. People might feel dizzy, sick to their stomachs, weak, angry, resentful. They might sweat a lot. People management helps people act in ways that will make the rescue less difficult, so there will be fewer injuries, damage, or confusion.

HOW do you do it? By controlling yourself and your own reactions, and then by: 1) identifying yourself; 2) being direct and honest; 3) allowing people to express their emotions; 4) forming a plan of action and sharing it; and 5) talking and touching. Most of your problems will arise through fear. If you can speak and move calmly, it will help everyone. Especially you.

48

Is the scene safe?

Keep away from anyone who makes you uncomfortable.

Violent, angry people full of rage and frustration may be more dangerous than the scene you are trying to manage.

Your own safety always comes first.

* * *

To learn more about people control, read *Fears and Phobias*, by Neal Olshan and Julie Wang. Published by Franklin Watts, 1980.

Emergency Rescue! Report

Report number 2	My name *Davey Mountain*

Incident location
Capitol Street
street
Augusta , Maine
city/town   state

My address
Sea Street
street
Camden , ME 04843
city/town   state   zip

Was the scene safe?   yes   no
Describe the scene.   ☒ ?   ☐

The elevator got stuck.

First name of victim Age male female	Aid first given by
most names unknown all ages ☒ ☒	☒ me *and Ma* ☐ someone else ☐ EMTs ☐ police ☐ firefighters

Transported to *fourth floor*

Describe any transportation
or communication problems.

none

Type of illness or injury or accident

☐ bone fracture
☐ aches and sprains
☐ bleeding injury
☐ illness
☐ fire
☐ auto or truck accident
☐ water incident
☐ HazMat
☐ airplane disaster
☐ lost person/search and rescue
☒ extrication
☐ animal incident
☐ electrical accident
☐ tornado
☐ hurricane
☐ blizzard
☐ other

Who called for help?

☒ me
☐ a friend
☐ family member
☐ professional
   responder
☐ neighbor
☐ other person

Emergency responders on the scene

☒ EMTs
☒ firefighters
☐ police
☐ HazMat
☐ emergency department
☐ utility crew
☐ search and rescue

Describe what happened, and the outcome. Include unusual
circumstances. *Nine people, including a pregnant lady*
were trapped between floors. While we waited for
the fire department, Matt and I kept the passenger
calm. We did a decent job but one man got sick
and one woman almost had a baby – actually
twins!! We don't know
their names.   my signature *Davey Mountain*

3
Spill

W*ho-o-om.*

Wind gusts hit the little red convertible as an Atlas Van Lines truck blew by.

Stacy Rich steadied her steering wheel.

She was driving her brother Matt and their cousin Davey to a pre-season hockey game at her old college, the University of Maine, in Orono.

Sprawled across the backseat was Matt, holding his book before his eyes. Physically, he was on a highway in Maine, in a cozy car, belted into his supple leather seat.

Mentally, he was into his book's wilderness story. He was reading *Hatchet*, a survival adventure about someone named Brian Robeson.

Not surprisingly, the book's boy-hero was in dan-

51

ger. Matt nibbled the cuticle on his right pointer finger as a bull moose whomped into Brian like a runaway truck.

Who-o-om!

Noise and bulk jerked Matt back to New England. A white tanker was overtaking them.

Davey dozed through the noise. He was riding shotgun, his Red Sox cap tugged down, and a Maine road map hanging off his lap.

Matt looked outside. Beyond the interstate, flame-colored Maine woodland opened. Fall. *Much like*, thought Matt, *Brian's forest.*

Hatchet drooped onto his MAINE HOCKEY sweatshirt.

The white Strick tanker downshifted, then rolled ahead. A blast of crosswind quivered the car's convertible top.

The tanker overtook a flatbed truck hauling drums of chemicals.

But not for long.

The flatbed veered into the passing lane.

Matt searched the oval back of the tanker for an oil company name or logo. But there was only a diamond-shaped hazard sign with numbers.

The flatbed took the lead. Truck leapfrog at seventy-five miles an hour.

Matt had no idea how hazardous the tanker or the flatbed were. Which got him wondering whether the drivers did either.

What were they hauling?

Dog-earing his page, he asked Davey, "Hand me your dad's HazMat book from the glove compartment, would you?"

Stacy changed lanes as her cousin passed the Department of Transportation guidebook of hazardous materials over the seat to Matt. The book was flame-orange colored.

My sister, Matt thought as he opened the book, *must be freaking out driving Aunt Jill and Uncle David's Saab in this heavy-duty traffic.* Their father had needed Stacy's VW bus to pick up a chopping block for Rich's Diner.

Matt thumbed the pages for the identification numbers of hazardous materials.

He looked back at the white tanker's placard.

It had a flame and **FLAMMABLE** in a red diamond. The number **9192** was in an orange rectangle beneath the diamond.

The guidebook said 9192, the truck's cargo, was fluorine. Like the stuff in refrigerators, in a car's air conditioner. Keeps things cold. Useful stuff.

He read the potential hazards of fluorine.

By now, both trucks were far ahead, barreling along.

Good, thought Matt, *because the liquid in that Strick tanker is poisonous and explosive. Worse, you couldn't taste or smell fluorine vapors. So how would you know where they were?*

You wouldn't.

If fluorine leaks, the immediate isolation distance is—Matt turned the page—*300 yards*. You'd be in danger if you were within three football fields of the spill. And once fluorine vapors begin to drift in the air, anyone within three miles downwind of the spill would have to leave.

Whoa.

Another tank truck was overtaking them, a Mack with a chrome bulldog guarding the hood. *Loaded with? 1017. Let's see . . . that's chlorine.*

"Davey, Stacy, listen to this . . ."

The car vibrated as the stainless steel tanker breezed by.

"You have to," Matt told them, "stay 900 feet from a small spill. If that truck crashes and the stuff leaks, then it says here to get back 1500 feet. And if you're downwind, where the wind's carrying the stuff toward you, you should clear out a five-mile-long and two-and-a-half-mile-wide area."

"If this guy was to lose it"—Matt looked out at the tanker—"we'd be in deep sneakers."

Davey and Stacy eyeballed the disappearing trucks.

Matt pondered traveling next to dynamite at highway speeds. Or worse. Dynamite would hurt or kill, but the danger would be over in one big boom.

Chemicals like chlorine and fluorine move on the wind. They're heavier than air so they settle in low areas. Walk into some depression in the land, and there's the HazMat—sitting in wait. Often you can't see it, feel it, or smell it.

"I've got to go to the bathroom," said Matt. "And hide maybe."

The environmental dangers of the road were a bummer.

* * *

In the truck stop, huge rigs parked left and right displaying HazMat placards. It made Matt nervous.

"Groan," agreed Davey.

The three walked toward Dude's Trucker Restaurant, passing rows of diesel pumps and a truck wash.

Matt peeked in at a tanker getting a shampoo. It was the bulldog Mack that had passed them on the road, the one with the chlorine payload.

Parked to the left of Dude's were a couple of bobtails—cabs without trailers.

Inside, the restaurant was a home away from home, truckers' style. There was a take-out snack area with packaged foods—pastrami sandwiches, Ritz Bits, fresh peaches, Pretzel Goldfish, and gourmet frozen yogurts for those truckers with mini-fridges in their cabs.

Off to the left, a TV blared *Oprah* in a living room-like area of stuffed chairs, coffee tables, ashtrays, and relaxing truckers. A sign above the television announced FOR TRUCKERS ONLY. There was an arrow pointing the way to showers.

On the right were dining booths, each with a phone for truckers. A smudged card in the wire loop of the salt and pepper rack, right above the Equal packets, said CREDIT CARD CALLS ONLY.

While Stacy and Davey ordered lunch, Matt went in search of a men's room for civilians.

He strolled by a bank of video games. Truckers were attacking them like raccoons on a bag of garbage.

Matt stopped at a counter with every sort of radar detector imaginable, and shelves of mud flaps, CDs, radios, and monster side-view mirrors.

"Can I help?" asked a gum-chewing saleswoman who wore her name on her uniform: DENISE.

"Just looking." Matt took off for the toilets.

*   *   *

By the time he got back to the booth, Matt's Dudeburger had arrived at the table.

So had a couple of young truckers, who were buzzing around Stacy like flies on a piece of lemon meringue pie.

The food was welcome. The truckers' attention wasn't.

Behind their booth sat an older trucker sucking barbecue sauce off his fingers. He pushed a plateful of bare ribs, a squished coleslaw cup, two curly fries, and an empty milk-coated glass.

The trucker wiped his hands on his jeans and reached out for the phone. He punched in a number, then his credit card code.

"Hey, hey, Shirl," his face was a tired grin. "How's my doll?"

Matt watched him rub his eyes.

"Hold it." He stopped the waitress passing by. "A large coffee, Penny? Three sugars. Thanks."

Matt pushed away his half-eaten Dudeburger.

"Stacy, let's rock 'n' roll." He worked on a piece of Dudeburger snagged on his braces. "Those jerks are gonna be drooling in my plate." His thumb stabbed toward the young truckers sitting nearby, flashing smiles and winks at his sister.

Matt stood to leave.

While Stacy recalculated the tip, he listened some more to the trucker on the phone, ". . . I've been on the road fifteen hours, doll, but you tell young Joel I'll keep on truckin'. Now don't you worry. I'm driving careful—you know we need that bonus I'll get for hauling hazardous cargo."

His fingers squeezed the bridge of his nose.

"I'll be there by noon tomorrow. Promise." He removed a bottle of pills from his pocket. Dex-A-Wake. "Yup, in time for his birthday party. Love you too, hon."

He hung up just as Penny brought the coffee.

* * *

Like a tributary flowing into the mighty Penobscot River, the jaunty red convertible merged with highway traffic.

Four top-heavy logging trucks trundled by, trav-

57

eling from Maine's ten million acres of commercial woodland. No doubt they were headed north to the Millinocket paper mills.

Stacy cruised the Mountains' Saab between the monster trucks. A ladybug in the land of giants.

Maybe, thought Matt, *those logs'll become milk cartons or a jillion toothpicks*. He said out loud, "That tired trucker we left back at the restaurant, the one driving that chlorine tanker? I bet he's taking it to the paper mills to Clorox the pulp."

Bits of sawdust cycloned in the wind.

Matt had read about ten pages of *Hatchet* when that same silver chlorine tanker pulled up. *What that driver needs*, thought Matt, *is a fluffy pillow and a bed. What he has are twelve gears and eighteen wheels. And a bomb*.

Matt closed his book. Brian Robeson had survived the moose, but his camp was wrecked by a ferocious wind.

Safer right here in Maine, he thought.

Or was it? Matt watched the Mack bulldog even up with his window as he fingered the end of his seat belt strap.

The truck driver looked down at him.

Does he recognize me from Dude's? Matt pulled an imaginary whistle cord.

The trucker blew his air horn. Then he put pedal to metal.

Matt, Davey, and Stacy sucked diesel fumes.

*　*　*

A half-hour later, the car's speakers were belting out Grateful Dead music.

Ahead, red brake lights were dominoing back. Along with the traffic around her, Stacy slowed.

She hit the brakes.

The passing-lane traffic kept moving.

Stacy stayed to the right, in the travel lane. The wilderness-first responder in her wondered about an accident up ahead.

The highway curved.

Between a green pickup and the scarlet maples lining the highway, was smoke.

Then the green pickup truck blocked their view. They read its bumper sticker — KEEP MAINE GREEN. SHOOT A DEVELOPER. — as it pulled off the road.

Stacy pressed her hazard light switch.

Behind her, three cars stopped.

Davey sat up, pushed his cap back. "Looks like we've got a situation here."

A thin plume of gray rose in the sky from what looked like a tanker far off the road.

Car doors opened.

A flannel-shirted man jumped from the pickup. "Did ja see that?" His words shot through his clenched cigar. "That tanker whizzed past me and missed the curve. Kept going clear across the breakdown lane. And," — he pointed with a hand that lacked two fingers — "look't it now. Godfrey ding-busted way over there in the puckerbrush."

* * *

There was a fresh scar on the land.

Matt's eye moved along the gouge. At the other end of the plowed-up land was the stainless steel oval of the tanker's rear.

Its jackknifed cab angled off.

Stacy turned to her cousin. "Davey, we passed an emergency phone maybe a quarter of a mile back. Can you run and activate the 9-1-1 system? Tanker off in the swamp. Possible HazMat. No information . . ."

Davey was booking down the highway's edge before she finished. ". . . on injuries. And stay out of the way of the cars!" she yelled after him.

"Matt" — she peered over the cattails toward the truck — "let's survey this scene."

* * *

The lumberjack started walking toward the tanker.

"Stop." He turned at Matt's command. "See that red diamond, sir? That's Haz-Mat — hazardous materials." Matt was on tiptoe, neck craned. "Can you read the number?"

"It's 1017." Matt echoed the man. "That's chlorine. *That's* the tanker that passed us."

The man's eyes ran from truck to kid and back to truck.

Through the haze they watched a hand fumble with the tanker's door handle.

60

"Looky there," the lumberjack cried. "We've got to get the guy out — he's gonna need doctoring. This standing here's about as productive as shearin' a pig."

A trickle of black smoke drifted from the tanker's engine compartment.

"No." Matt sniffed. "We need to move *further* away. I think I smell bleach."

The lumberjack spit out his cigar. "I don't smell nothing." He rubbed his nose against his flannel sleeve. "Well, maybe a whiff. . . . But how's about that driver? You just said it's dangerous. He's gotta get out."

Stacy jumped in. "No. My brother's right. Dead heroes don't save lives. The driver's on his own. Until HazMat personnel arrive."

A piece of the lumberjack wanted to be a lifesaver.

The other part of him wanted to stay alive.

Matt made eye contact. "Look, sir. We might have a chlorine spill on our hands. You walk into the gas, it'll be all over. That stuff is a chemical warfare component. If the engine catches fire and the burn spreads to the tank, vapors'll explode. *Serious* HazMat incident."

As he spoke, he walked backward, the lumberjack following.

* * *

A tow truck slowed and pulled over.

"Matt," Stacy touched her brother's shoulder, "I'm

61

gonna ask the guy driving that hooker" — she pointed at the tow truck — "to radio in the tanker's cargo. See if you can keep these folks back."

Two teenagers, a man in a business suit with his tie loosened, and a couple with a toddler were standing back on the hardtop. "What have we got here?" they asked as Matt walked up. "What happened?"

"Tanker hauling chlorine," answered Matt. "And there's smoke coming from the engine. My cousin called it in back at the roadside emergency phone."

"Jeezum," said the toddler's mother. "Where's the driver? Still in the rig?"

"Aha, that *is* bleach we smelled," said the taller of the two teens, the one with the tie-dyed Earth Day T-shirt. "Is it organic? What'll happen to the wetland?"

"Never mind the wetland," said Matt. "Our lungs are at risk."

He looked at the rising smoke. He couldn't see the chlorine and its movement, but knew it would be blown by the wind. Like the smoke but lower down, because it was heavier.

"We've got to back off about twice as far as we are now from the tanker. Another four hundred fifty feet at least." *If the wind shifts this way*, he thought, *we'll have to move even further.*

Right now, he'd be glad to see any movement from this bunch.

"Let's go for it, man," said the freckled teen, who started walking back toward his car. "I'm with this kid."

"And how," questioned the businessman with eyebrow raised, "did your cousin tell them where we are?" He waved his arm at the emptiness surrounding them.

"I believe the phone does that, sir. The 9-1-1 system pinpoints the call's origination."

"But," the toddler's mom was talking to the others, "how can we abandon the driver? It's terrible. If that were me . . ."

She looked back at the darkening sky.

Three people answered her, all with different ideas. If they kept discussing it, Matt knew they'd never get around to any action.

How *was* that driver doing?

"Come oooon." Freckleface had become Matt's lieutenant. "Let's all wait behind that dirty gray Toyota." He looked at Matt. "Will that do it?"

Oddly, everyone stopped arguing. And moved. Including the lumberjack.

Matt looked to the sky. The smoke was black and drifting fast, but not in their direction. His shoulders felt lighter. They rose and fell as he sighed.

He turned around and booked it back to the others.

* * *

Crashing through brush and boulders had been rough on driver and tanker.

The windshield was spidered.

The steering wheel was gone. Its post tilted at a crazy angle.

The driver's seat had come off its mountings.

The glove compartment was open and emptied. All the loose things which had been tucked in special places were littered on the floor, on the dash, over the seat. Every horizontal surface was covered with dirty, broken junk.

A single work boot lay on its side on the passenger seat. Its laces were still tied.

Within the damaged cab, there was a stir.

The truck driver was still seat-belted, and the straps held him half up. His forehead was purpled and angry-looking.

There was a jagged tear down the left side of his shirt. The corduroy was soaking up blood dripping from where his ribs had hit the door handle.

The handle was gone.

There was no sound in the cab except for a menacing hiss. Escaping chlorine gas?

The driver opened one eye. It felt as if it had nail polish remover in it. He closed it, and tried to think about what he'd been able to see.

A wave of pain hit. He stopped thinking.

Back again. A steady flow of smoke was blowing in through the windshield. *So hard to concentrate. Electrical fire in the engine compartment? Maybe worse if leaking gas starts hitting the overheated engine block.*

His eyes stayed closed.

Minutes went by. Or hours. The driver heard sobbing, thought someone else was there until he realized it was his own cries.

Sniff. *What's that?* Sniff, sniff? *Familiar, but strange, too. Acrid. Different from the smoke smell. Overpowering. Burning my throat.*

The chlorine. Jesus! The chlorine. Got to get out of here. Got to do it NOW.

His right hand fumbled with the seat belt latch. He felt his body shake, as if laughing at his problem. Strange how a normal movement gets tough all of a sudden. Impossible, in fact. Another slow try with a right arm and hand finally landed the ball of his thumb on the button. Four fingers underneath to push and lift.

The belt popped open and away.

Hard to breathe. Lungs aren't working right. Feel like I'm drowning. Got to let go. Got to sleep.

No! Get out. Now. The door. Have to open it.

Fumble for the handle. *Can't find it. My eyes are killing me. Maybe if I rest — rest for just a second — maybe then I'll be able to figure a way out.*

But where the handle was supposed to be there was now a jagged piece of metal and a tear in the vinyl upholstery. The handle was over by the CB, lying between the radio and windshield.

Got to get out. It hurts to breathe. . . .

The truck driver paused; the chlorine and the fire didn't. They gathered in strength.

One eye opened a slit.

This was going to be his last chance to get out of the truck. Last chance, period.

The fumbling left hand found the outside handle. The only way to move it was to take his whole hand, wedge it under, then pry out.

And pray.

The latch clicked and the door opened, a crack. But it moved.

Time to rest, for just a second. Then lean hard against the door.

Now!

The door sprung open and the top half of the trucker's body fell out. One stockinged foot hung up in a tangle of seat track and brake pedal. Twist, grunt. *Pull on the leg. But it hurts. A lot.*

There, untangled.

The driver tumbled the last sixteen inches into the swamp. *Sweet grass.*

The cold water shocked him. Just enough strength and energy to get up and run.

No thoughts; no plans. Run as if life depends on it. Can't pay attention to feeling that it takes two, three breaths to get enough oxygen to keep alive. And even that's not enough, never enough.

Move!

Got to keep moving. Fifty, sixty, seventy feet. Hopping, limping, and stumbling.

Finally out of the swamp and into a brushy meadow.

There's a ragged gap in the turnpike fence — how'd that get there? Toward a group of people standing by the road. *It's like they're a hundred miles away. But I can see them, right over there. Why are they staring? Don't they see how I'm running?*

Why won't they help me? Why do they just stand there?

* * *

Matt and Stacy watched the truck driver struggle through swamp and field. From the moment the man had fallen from the cab, it had been tough to not help.

It was agony watching his progress.

A snail's pace. A movie in slow motion, and getting slower by the minute.

Nobody in the watching group had spoken, but they were all thinking the same thing. *If he's alive, then the chlorine vapors can't be such a big deal. What harm would there be in running down there to help? Real quick. Maybe hold your breath?*

Stacy put her arm around Matt's shoulders.

Matt kept reviewing in his mind all that he knew about HazMat, all that Chief Oxton, back in Camden, had told him. *Secure the scene — get people out of the contamination zone. Limit exposure. Wait for professionals to aid the injured.*

He watched the trucker. It looked like he had broken his lower leg, a tibia or fibula fracture. At least. Maybe the femur, his thigh looked unnatural. Matt shifted his weight off his bad knee.

Where was *the HazMat team from Hampden?* The sound of sirens answered his question.

* * *

An instant after Matt heard the fire and HazMat trucks, there was a strange new sound, coming from the direction of the tanker.

The Earth Day teenager gasped.

Pouring from the cab was smoke, now muddied brown, gray, and blue. The cloud covered most of the smashed windshield and open door.

There was a flicker — orange flame here, red and blue there. Then the cab was engulfed. Matt was reminded of a Chinese New Year fire-breathing, papier-mâché dragon. The whole truck seemed to snort, belch smoke, and toss about.

The gasoline tank went with a boom bigger than a thousand firecrackers.

No matter that the chlorine tank was made of heavy-gauge steel. No matter that the valve assembly was protected from collision by a shield. Fire got to the chlorine. The gas escaping from the cracked valve under the belly of the tanker caught and burned like a blow torch, the flame running up both sides of the steel tanker.

The hazardous materials placard melted under the flames' attack.

Chlorine, already under extreme pressure, heated, and expanded further. Steel welding parted, the tank shattered.

The chlorine was out.

The explosion which followed dwarfed the gas tank explosion. A fire ball rolled out, lost energy, and began to rise.

Then it turned into smoke — white, green, rust, yellow billows.

An ashed piece of placard floated to the ground at Matt's feet. He felt his heart beat.

The trucker didn't take in the blaze and the blasts, though the power of the chlorine explosion flattened him. The heat washed over him and then was gone.

He got up, hopped another step. Fell. Then crawled. He kept moving forward, aching to breathe. Finding it difficult to focus his vision on the group of people and cars in the distance.

* * *

"Please move back behind the plastic tape. There are toxic fumes present. Move back."

From behind, Matt, Davey, Stacy, and the others watched two HazMat responders cinch on air tanks and face masks for their Self-Contained Breathing

Apparatus. Then they donned full encapsulating gear — cocoons — taping the seams air-tight.

They approached the driver, using their SCBA to breathe. Everyone watched.

The driver never saw them coming. But as soon as he felt their hands under his armpits and heard their words, some inner voice allowed him to give up the struggle.

He lost consciousness.

The CHLOREP rescuers — the chlorine industry's emergency planning team — moved quickly. The trucker was carried to the designated control zone, out of the contaminated area.

Matt and Davey watched from the safe zone, behind the tape.

First, an oxygen mask was placed over the driver's face. His eyes were flushed with fluids from a hand-held irrigation bag. Every so often an EMT would remove the oxygen mask, and suction bloody froth from the man's mouth and nose.

That was when Matt saw how blue his skin was. Cyanotic. Lack of oxygen.

As the unconscious man was wheeled to an ambulance, Stacy walked along. "Pulmonary edema?" she asked, after identifying herself as a professional rescuer.

"He's bad," whispered the EMT. "Dyspnea. Listen to that wheeze. But he's breathing easier already. We'll pull him through. Be a long time, though, till he's up to driving a truck again. If ever."

Stacy helped the men lift the cot into the ambulance.

"How'd you manage to contain the spectators?" the CHLOREP EMT asked her.

"My brother took charge," she said, pointing at Matt.

"Good man," the medic responded.

* * *

A truck overtook the little red ragtop as it motored toward Orono and U-Maine's hockey rink.

Inside the truck's HazMat diamond was **1203**.

As they hung a right onto the exit ramp and tooled along at a good clip, Davey opened his father's *Emergency Response Guidebook*. "Gasoline, according to the book. Hmmmm. Listen. 'Isolate for one-half mile in all directions if truck is involved in fire. . . .'"

Skill
HazMat Response

WHAT is it? Ensuring HazMat bystander safety.

WHY do you do it? There are hidden dangers in hazardous materials. Matt protected folks who didn't know the dangers.

WHEN do you do it? Whenever you find a possible hazardous materials accident. Even before Matt was sure there was a chlorine spill, he kept people and himself at a safe distance.

HOW do you do it? By thinking calmly and logically. 1) Always stay upwind from the incident. 2) Move people away from site, and don't let new arrivals come close. 3) Do not walk into or touch any spilled material. 4) Don't inhale smoke or vapors. Ash and burning debris give off toxic fumes. Although these materials may not be considered HazMat, they damage lung tissue and other parts of your body. Keep away. 5) Don't think gases or vapors are harmless just because they don't smell. Some of the worst chemicals are odorless.

Is the scene safe?
Never endanger yourself trying to herd people

back. Matt walked back himself, even when the lumberjack would not.

If you are the first on the scene, activate the EMS system. You can also call the emergency Chemtrec number 800/424-9300. In Alaska and Washington, D.C., call collect 202/483-7616.

* * *

To learn more about HazMat response, read *Emergency Response Guidebook*, published by the U.S. Department of Transportation, 1990.

Emergency Rescue! Report

Report number 3	My name MATT RICH

Incident location	My address
ROUTE 95	BAY VIEW STREET
street NEAR	street
HAMPDEN MAINE	CAMDEN, ME. 04843
city/town state	city/town state zip

Was the scene safe?   yes   no BECAUSE THE TANKER WAS
Describe the scene.   ☐   ☒ LEAKING CHLORINE GAS,
THERE WAS DANGER FROM POISON AND EXPLOSION.
EVERYONE HAD TO STAY BACK AND WATCH THE WIND.

First name of victim Age male female	Aid first given by
DON'T KNOW ? ☒ ☐	☐ me
	☒ someone else
Transported to	☐ EMTs HAZ
SOME HOSPITAL	☐ police M
	☐ firefighters

Describe any transportation MY COUSIN HAD TO
or communication problems. RUN BACK DOWN
THE HIGHWAY TO USE AN EMERGENCY PHONE.

Type of illness or injury or accident	Who called for help?
☒ bone fracture	☐ me
☒ aches and sprains	☒ a friend DAVEY
☐ bleeding injury	☐ family member
☒ illness- HIS LUNGS WERE MESSED UP	☐ professional
☐ fire BY THE GAS.	responder
☒ auto or truck accident	☐ neighbor
☐ water incident	☐ other person
☒ HazMat	
☐ airplane disaster	**Emergency responders on**
☐ lost person/search and rescue	**the scene**
☐ extrication	☒ EMTs
☐ animal incident	☒ firefighters
☐ electrical accident	☐ police
☐ tornado	☒ HazMat
☐ hurricane	☐ emergency department
☐ blizzard	☐ utility crew
☐ other	☐ search and rescue

Describe what happened, and the outcome. Include unusual
circumstances. WE SAW IT AFTER THE CRASH. ALL WE
COULD DO WAS WATCH THE DRIVER GET AWAY FROM
THE TRUCK BEFORE IT EXPLODED. WE KNEW TO KEEP
OURSELVES AND OTHERS AWAY FROM THE TOXIC GAS.
THE HAZMAT RESPONDERS SAID I DID A GOOD JOB.

my signature *Matt Rich*

4
Sting

Susan Baer bent over and removed a pebble from the toe of her sandal. She turned the mineral over and around in her palm.

As Susan examined the stone, Davey Mountain looked at her. She had this habit of putting her gold MedicAlert necklace between her lips when she concentrated.

The pendant fell from her mouth as she licked the tiny piece of granite. "Not salty," she announced. "No sodium."

Davey rolled his eyes.

Susan was new to Maine and had never been on the rugged island of Monhegan. *Everything* fascinated her.

Which was one of the reasons why Davey liked her.

Which he didn't always understand. . . .

At first he hadn't thought of Susan when his parents said he could bring a friend to Monhegan for the weekend.

But it was a holiday and the start of the tourist season, so Davey's best friend and cousin, Matt Rich, had to wash dishes in his parents' restaurant.

Stacy, who managed Rich's Diner while her dad and mom cooked, said she couldn't do without her brother Matt.

In fact, she tried to convince Davey to work, too.

But Davey wanted to get in some spring kayaking. He and Susan, who lived opposite him on Sea Street, had talked half the winter about getting out on the water.

So he asked Susan to come to Monhegan.

She'd said yes.

As they walked along the island road, gravel crunched beneath their feet. The noise stopped as Susan paused in front of the island's ambulance. ". . . I don't get it." Her deep voice always sounded like it came from the back of the closet. "An island with three beat-up trucks and a handful of year-round families. One dirt road. . . . And an ambulance?"

"Mmmm, I know," he said. "And I bet most rescues here are in the woods or on the cliffs, so really it's — " In the middle of his sentence, a deer appeared at the edge of the road.

Its Bambi eyes watched them.

Davey glanced from the doe to across the harbor at tiny Manana Island, a Frisbee-throw away.

That's where the Mountains and Susan were staying for the long weekend, along with Bossy, the Mountains' pet.

If you didn't count the lighthouse, there was one dwelling on Manana — the half-built house the Riches and the Mountains were working on. No phone. Kerosene lantern time. Really, it was camping out.

Sometimes a deer would swim over from Monhegan. But mostly Manana belonged to a flock of sheep who grazed the island, and to Davey and Matt's families who traveled there from Camden whenever they could.

The day before, the Mountains and Susan had come over from the mainland. The first leg of their trip had been a one-hour lobster boat ride to Monhegan. Then the four of them rowed over to Manana. The bulldog, Bossy, commandeered the bow thwart in the double-ended peapod, checking out all the delightful new smells as his jowls flapped in the breeze.

Washington crossing the Delaware.

* * *

Before the influx of summer folk, the Monhegan Store opened for business at noon, after the mail boat's arrival.

Davey and Susan, the day's first customers, walked in to buy picnic food. Davey wanted a Monhegan trail map.

Outside again, he stowed their purchases in the daypack next to his Toblerone bar and Susan's bee-sting injector. Then they headed for the harbor.

Around them, trees were greening out with spring.

As they walked, Davey went back to their Monhegan ambulance conversation. "Really, that ambulance is a field hospital for MERS — that's what the Monhegan Emergency Rescue Service calls itself. The rig gives the island EMTs a place to store gear, and check out patients. Til a boat takes 'em to Port Clyde.

"Then a mainland ambulance meets the lobster boat, and transports the person up to Penobscot Bay Hospital."

Ahead of them, a lone lobster boat bobbed at a granite pier.

Beyond was Fish Beach, dotted with turned-over dinghies. It was the dory landing used by Monhegan fishermen who rowed out to their boats in the harbor.

Wedged between the pier and the bold shore, the little beach looked embarrassed. A sandpiper poked a tangle of kelp, a fiddler crab darted under a granite boulder. Ospreys cut swirls in the sky.

From somewhere off in Deadman's Cove a loon cried, while behind Duck Rock a pair of eiders worked the mussel beds as if there were no tomorrow.

They were wrong: This first spring day promised plenty of tomorrows.

Davey and Susan frogged their waiting kayak over the sand and into the frigid water. As they waded around rocks, Susan handled the heft of the boat.

Davey liked that about her. A tough female.

But he didn't want to think about that. What he wanted to do was set his adjustable seat, straighten the back rest and get out on the water.

Balancing his weight on both gunwales, he pivoted into the double kayak's stern.

He turned his Red Sox cap so the visor faced backwards, as Susan push-upped her body into the bow, behind the forward cargo hatch.

She made it look easy.

Davey's paddle, the length of a Ping-Pong table, broke the surface of the water.

As he danced its double ends — in and out, in and out — he got his rhythm from Susan. Following her cadence, their kayak slit the blue-black water, ghosting past the lobster boat at the granite pier.

A high school kid was off-loading green wire lobster traps onto the wharf. He straightened, noting their progress.

Bobbed his head.

The kayak sliced through the harbor. Davey and the boat's sleek form were all one thing, with Susan a piece of it, too.

Their paddles swept them along. Davey, kayak, water, Susan.

The sun felt great.

I'll remember this moment for the rest of my life, Davey promised himself.

As they slid through the gut between Smutty Nose Island and Monhegan, Davey looked back over his left shoulder toward Manana.

He could make out a couple of figures that were his parents.

He saw Mom wave a handful of papers. They must be settling down in the sun to rework their latest manuscript.

Davey touched Susan's shoulder with the blade of his paddle, then pointed toward the top of one of Manana's two ridges.

Against the sky, there was Bossy in a face-off with a ram. Who was king of the hill?

Susan did her throaty chuckle.

They glided around the spit at the end of Deadman's Cove.

Ahead lay Seal Ledges. As they neared, what appeared to be rocks became seals, hauled out to warm and dry in the early afternoon sun.

Davey, paddling along, imagined he was the greatest jock there ever was. His kayak was perfectly balanced. He was the strong agile oarsman. *They should film this for a Mountain Dew commercial.*

* * *

"I'm hungry," announced Susan, always eager to tie on the feedbag. The sun was now high in the sky. "Wanna pull up to that pile of rocks over there and scarf down a sandwich or two?"

Food never tasted better. It was a Monhegan kind of day.

After lunch, they sunned themselves like the seals.

Susan split the last two sections of tangerine and shared with Davey.

He popped the fruit into his mouth, then groped around for the day pack. He held it up over his chest and zipped open the front pocket.

Susan turned her head at the rustle of a candy wrapper. By sound alone, she could tell a Snickers from a Mars.

Davey lifted his head and turned to her. "Toblerone." His addiction. "Swiss chocolate."

"Is it high fat?" Susan sucked in her stomach. "What's in it?"

His eyes squinted. "There's *chocolat au lait suisse avec nougat au miel et aux amandes.*"

"*Eh bien.*" Susan sat next to Davey in French. "*Donnez moi en peu?*"

He propped on his elbow, snapped off a triangle-shaped piece and handed it to her.

She swallowed the candy. "I have absolutely no will power. I love this chocolate. *Excusez moi, chocolat.*"

Davey knew that Susan wanted to get rid of all her baby fat. But that wouldn't make her look better to him. She was a neat person, great to be with.

The sun, the Toblerone. *Maybe,* he thought as he sponged up rays, *when we get back we can poke around the lighthouse.*

Then tomorrow, he planned as he drifted into sleep, *paddle around the other end of the island, haul out in Christmas Cove, and climb the cliffs.*

* * *

Susan stirred, rubbing her temple with the back of her hand.

She opened her eyes. "Davey, we ought to get out of this sun. Any of that *chocolat* left? To jump-start my pecs for the paddle back."

He rooted around in the daypack, broke the last piece of chocolate in half.

He tossed some to Susan and seagulled down the remainder.

Susan bit off the corner of her candy.

She flicked an insect away from her forehead.

Davey searched the air around her hair. "That's a honey bee. This early in the year they're rare as a freshwater lobster. Bee's got good taste, wanting Toblerone."

Still on her back, Susan fingered her MedicAlert necklace, with its ALLERGIC TO BEE STINGS. She nibbled, her senses on red-alert for buzzing insects.

"Wanna go?" Davey asked. The bee was bothering

Susan, he could see. Besides, his shoulders had had enough sun.

Susan sat up as she popped the remainder of the candy into her mouth.

"Ummmph!"

She spit out unchewed chocolate. "I think I've been stung . . . maybe on my tongue."

Davey saw tears well in the corners of her eyes, from pain.

"Stick out your tongue."

It was huge. So soon a reaction. He searched for the stinger. He couldn't see it.

Susan's body was freaking out from the bee venom.

Susan's tongue filled her mouth, making it hard to breathe.

The last time she was stung she'd almost died from such an anaphylactic reaction. *And*, Davey thought to himself, *each time is worse than the last.*

I got, he decided, *a situation here.*

Now, within seconds, Susan's microscopic cell-defense team had again flooded her body with something called histamine.

The chemical histamine souped up her insides so her cells could slide by one another as they attacked the invading bee poison.

Which made sense.

Except some people, like Susan, reacted too much. Their defense system tried to wipe out a mosquito with a bomb.

Overkill.

Bee venom wouldn't kill Susan. Her body's over-reaction would.

Out on some puny island. Worse, on some rocks next to a kayak. No one to help.

He felt stunned.

Then sprang into action.

* * *

The kayak bobbed in the water.

"Move," he ordered Susan, grabbing the daypack and unzipping it.

She crawled in the boat.

Her face was a mask of fear, red and puffy. Tears streamed over her cheeks. Her nose was running. The histamine was doing its job.

She tried to talk.

"Bu-u vee needooo. . . ." Susan's tongue was making it hard for her to pronounce words. Her strong voice was weak, and she was having trouble catching her breath.

She gave up, laid her head back, closed her eyes.

Ever since her reaction to that last bee sting, Susan carried medicine to protect her from her own cell defenses. Her bee-sting injector could save her life by buying time to get to an emergency department.

Davey uncapped the tube. The cap fell from his hand into the water. It drifted away. Stupidly, he stood and watched it.

"Daaa-vey." He almost couldn't hear her words.

"I know. Oh, I know, Susan. You need some epi."
He pulled the drug epinephrine from its tube. "We're cool. No problem."

What a joke, he said to himself.

"You're going to be fine." *I hope.*

He churned through the water over to Susan.

Her chest was rising and falling with each gurgling wheeze. He looked at her face, distorted with hives. Her lungs, filling with fluid, were checking out.

The epi in the injector would fight to keep open the tubes in her chest that were tightening. It would keep her heart beating so that blood continued to move through her body.

Davey held the injector in his left hand, wiped the sweat off the palm of his right.

Steadying the boat, Davey poised the injector over her thigh.

One, two . . .

A drop of perspiration fell from his forehead onto Susan's white shorts.

Got to push this down and hold it against her thigh. Needle into her skin, through to her muscle. Do it. DO IT!!!

. . . three.

The injector did its thing. The unseen needle, hidden in soft plastic, pierced her skin. He stared, then shook himself.

A wave of relief swept over him. At having done it? At the drug now inside Susan, saving her life?

85

Yes.

She picked up her head, looked at him. Her smile attempt was distorted. She didn't even try to speak. He was sure her throat was swollen. If it closed and she couldn't exchange air, she would suffocate.

Then — Davey almost couldn't think it — she'd die.

"Susan, I'm going to get you back, to get help. You try to relax, and breathe normal." *Just breathe. Any old way.* "Hey, you're okay. . . ."

He hoped she believed him.

* * *

It took forever to paddle the kayak back to the harbor.

All along the way, Davey's eyes searched for signs of life in the boarded-up summer houses lining the shore.

Nothing.

He passed Smutty Nose Island, and cut hard toward the beach landing, flailing his paddle. Frantic to see his stepmother or father — even Bossy — he glanced toward Manana.

"Here we go, Suse. We're almost there. You're doing great. . . ."

By the time he was lined up with the end of the pier, he was drenched with sweat. The muscles in his body were screaming.

"Hang on. That's right, keep breathing. I'm taking care of you. . . ."

Susan was slumped forward, shivering. Her only movement a shallow rise and fall of her back.

He had to paddle, get her to help.

It was driving him crazy to be so near, but unable to reach her. Should he lay his paddle down, crawl from his seat in the stern across the middle of the kayak and up to her? But what if he fell into the water? Then they'd be in a mess.

Paddle!

At the pier, the high school kid was about done helping the captain unload the traps.

"Hey," Davey called. "Help! I've got an emergency here. Bee sting. She's conscious and breathing, but we need help. Call MERS."

The high school boy froze in mid-step. Then sprung into action.

He grabbed something black, jumped over the boat's gunwale and landed sprinting to the beach — all the while talking into what Davey finally realized was a Monhegan Emergency Rescue Service portable radio.

The boat captain stared until his gaze caught Davey and the slumped-over Susan.

"Just keep breathing," Davey said as the kayak grounded on Fish Beach.

The high school kid pulled the boat up by its bow.

"In and out, in and out, breathe," Davey coached Susan as he helped drag the boat. "Hey, Suse, here we are now. The MERS EMTs are on their way."

The thought of professionals taking over was wonderful.

The high school kid knelt down next to Susan. He picked up her hand, his fingers on her wrist over her radial pulse. His radio squawked: "Portables Two and Six to Junior One. We're Ten-10 at the rig, picking up gear. Verify the *Evelyn C.* lobster boat standing by for transport. Copy anaphylactic female, conscious and disoriented. We'll be Ten-08 for Fish Beach. Then ready to rock 'n' roll. Ten-03? . . ."

Susan passed out.

* * *

The unconscious Susan had been lifted out of the kayak with the help of the lobster boat boy, a junior member of MERS. Her feet were propped on a rock and her head was downhill to encourage blood flow to her brain.

"Good positioning," said Trevor, one of the two MERS EMTs who arrived on the beach.

As Trevor spoke, his huge round face, the size of a dart board, was already on Susan. He unzipped a jumpkit. Out came a blood pressure cuff, oxygen tank, and a run pad.

Barbara, the other EMT, asked their junior member, "Got a radial?"

Davey tucked in the denim work shirt that lay over Susan.

Barbara tilted Susan's chin up in the air and slid a lubricated tube down her nose.

An airway was established. Oxygen was hooked up. "Run that O$_2$ flush," Barbara instructed.

Davey turned the wrench on the oxygen cylinder as far to the left as it would go. *Hiiiisssssss*. The EMT's eyebrows raised. She checked the green tank's gauge, gave Davey a thumbs-up look, and turned back to Susan.

Now the goal was transporting the patient off-island and to Penobscot Bay Hospital. Stat.

* * *

Aboard the lobster boat *Evelyn C.*, Davey repeated his radio message to MERS dispatch on Monhegan. "That's Jill and David Mountain. I'm Davey Mountain. They're on Manana. . . . Ten-04.

"Ask 'em to notify Susan's father. Susan'll get to the hospital at approximately 1600 hours. Over."

He handed the mike back to Captain Chandler.

"This is the *Evelyn C., Evelyn C.* to Camden marine operator." Once Camden acknowledged, Captain Chandler asked to be patched through to Penobscot Bay Hospital's radio.

When the hospital's dispatcher was on the line, the captain gave the mike to Trevor who reported Susan's condition: "We are *en route* to your facility with an unconscious female patient whose chief complaint is anaphylactic shock. . . ."

Behind Trevor, out in the middle of the boat's cabin-sole, lay Susan's stretcher.

Davey huddled over to protect her from the salt spray.

On the other side of the cot, Barbara slid an IV

needle into a vein on the back of Susan's hand.

Davey watched for Susan's response. She didn't flinch.

Davey held the IV bag up for Barbara. Fluid ran down through a tube and into Susan's hand vein.

The clear Ringer's solution, about the same makeup as the salt water in her body, would flush her insides clean of the histamine. And it would add fluid to replace liquid that had leaked out into the rest of her body.

EMTs Barbara and Trevor talked between themselves. "Look," Trevor said, "a paramedic could inject more epi. I think Susan needs it. And an antihistamine."

"Let's see," nodded Barbara as she reached for the radio, "if Tom Justice's available."

* * *

Within five minutes, EMT-paramedic Justice had sped, red light flashing, to the Port Clyde pier on the mainland.

He boarded a waiting speedboat and was at sea in minutes.

On the *Evelyn C.* everyone began watching for him long before it was possible to sight him. Either Davey's eyes were sharper or his need greater — in any event, it was he who first spotted the boat.

Once on board the lobster boat, Tom surveyed his patient and injected medications into Susan's IV line.

Now it was a question of waiting for the drugs to take effect. If they weren't too late.

Justice poured himself coffee, strong enough to float the boat, from Captain Chandler's thermos.

As he sipped and talked with Trevor and Barbara, Davey sat by Susan.

Just when he decided her swelling had gone down some, her eyes opened.

They zeroed in on Davey. She opened her mouth to speak.

"Tom!" Davey half-turned his head toward the paramedic without taking his eyes off Susan.

"Tom, she's awake!"

If Davey looked away, he might lose her again.

*   *   *

The wharf was in sight.

Three Port Clyde EMTs waited on the dock. Davey threw them the *Evelyn C.*'s line.

Susan's stretcher was wheeled the few feet to the waiting ambulance.

Inside the rig, Davey hovered. "Suse, I promised to call your dad as soon as you're on your way. Then I've got to go back. If I don't get on the *Evelyn C.* now, I won't be able to get to Monhegan at all.

"You know," he added, "I wouldn't leave you unless I was sure you're fine now. Right?"

She reached up and touched his cheek.

91

SKILL
Anaphylaxis Management

WHAT is it? Knowing how to spot anaphylaxis and acting when you see it. Anaphylaxis is when your whole body over-reacts to something you eat or breathe in, or something injected into you, like bee venom.

WHY do you do it? Allergic people have a life-or-death reaction and can't take care of themselves. So *you* must. If they don't get medical help, they may die.

WHEN do you do it? Right away. 1) Breathing problems are a tip-off. Remember how Susan wheezed as her throat closed? Do you see the signs of an allergy — hives, itching, rash — showing up everywhere on the body? Susan was stung on her tongue, but her whole face swelled. That's anaphylaxis. Weakness, nausea, vomiting, or dizziness are other signs. 2) If you aren't sure if an allergic reaction is anaphylaxis, *assume that it is*. 3) Activate the 9-1-1 system. Anaphylaxis kills in minutes.

HOW do you do it? After activating the 9-1-1 system, keep the patient warm and as comfortable as possible. Let her find the position that makes it easiest to breathe. Then raise her feet. If the person has an epinephrine injector, make sure it is used.

92

Is the scene safe?

Is the scene safe *for you*? Because of the risk of infection, the used needle in an epinephrine injector is dangerous. Once the epi has been injected, place the injector back in its plastic tube.

When the EMTs arrive, ask them to throw it away in their sharps box, where used needles are discarded.

* * *

To learn more about anaphylaxis management, read *Itch, Sniffle & Sneeze* by Dr. Alvin Silverstein and Virginia Silverstein. Published by Four Winds Press, 1978.

Emergency Rescue! Report

Report number	4	My name _Davey Mountain_

Incident location	My address
Seal Ledges	_Sea Street_
street	street
Monhegan Island, Maine	_Camden, ME 04843_
city/town state	city/town state zip

Was the scene safe?   yes   no
Describe the scene.   ☒   ☐

Susan and I were picnicking on the rocks, far away from everything.

First name of victim	Age	male	female	Aid first given by
Susan	13	☐	☒	☒ me ☐ someone else ☐ EMTs ☐ police ☐ firefighters

Transported to _Fish Beach by me, Port Clyde by boat, hospital by ambulance._

Describe any transportation or communication problems. _I had to transport her by kayak._

Type of illness or injury or accident

- ☐ bone fracture
- ☐ aches and sprains
- ☐ bleeding injury
- ☒ illness _bee sting_
- ☐ fire
- ☐ auto or truck accident
- ☐ water incident
- ☐ HazMat
- ☐ airplane disaster
- ☐ lost person/search and rescue
- ☐ extrication
- ☐ animal incident
- ☐ electrical accident
- ☐ tornado
- ☐ hurricane
- ☐ blizzard
- ☐ other

Who called for help?

- ☒ me
- ☐ a friend
- ☐ family member
- ☒ professional _junior MERS_ responder _member_
- ☐ neighbor
- ☐ other person

Emergency responders on the scene

- ☒ EMTs
- ☐ firefighters
- ☐ police
- ☐ HazMat
- ☐ emergency department
- ☐ utility crew
- ☐ search and rescue

Describe what happened, and the outcome. Include unusual circumstances. _When Susan got stung, I knew she was allergic but I didn't know how bad. Her tongue swelled up. I gave her an epi shot. She is fine now but both of us were real scared._

my signature _Davey Mountain_

5
Search

My first overnight with the Outing Club and I can just hear 'em, Matt thought. *'What a joke! — Matt Rich got himself lost.'*

But I didn't.

Maybe mixed up.

I'm not lost, Matt said to himself. *Naw. Todd'll be back here in a flash. He knows where I am. He's president of the Outing Club, knows his way around the woods. No big deal.*

Except that the guys back at camp are gonna get on my case.

Where is Todd? Matt wondered for the thousandth time.

Matt knew he had done the right thing once he realized they were in trouble.

'Find a space; show your face.' That's what the wardens always say. *But that's going to sound stupid with Todd already back at the base camp, goofing off. Laughing at me. Dragging out the time before he comes and gets me.*

And here I sit in the middle of the woods. . . .

Alone.

For a moment, reality was too cold.

Matt stared through a break in the pea-soup fog at what was maybe White Cap Mountain.

He wished Portable-D were there. His cousin Davey'd be sure to have a map and compass.

But he was the one who was this year's Outing Club junior member.

And he was the one who screwed up. Matt snorted. *Lost. On the first day.*

He zipped his windbreaker up tight, hunched his shoulders.

He blew into his hands and, with straight fingers, made heat by rubbing one palm against the other.

Ever since Todd left, Matt had sat in the same spot, dead in the middle of a clearing. Thinking. Talking to himself. And reading his book.

Once he got up, to leave clues. His deep footprints were cast in mud alongside the stream over to his left. And then he wrote his name there — MATT — carving two-foot letters with a pointed stick.

He looked down at his Merrell Rugged Walkers. His

dad had bought them for him, special for this trip.

They were twin mud balls.

Big, tough Matt cried. Without noise. First time since he mashed his knee. *Oh, yeah, except for that day Queenie died.*

Die?

Calm down Matt, he told himself, wiping his nose. So what if they hadn't found him yet? They would. The thing was to have a plan for what he was doing while he waited.

I ought to think over how I got here in the first place. . . .

* * *

For as long as Matt could remember — back to when his sister Stacy had been a member — the Windjammer School's Outing Club held its annual camping experience in northern Maine.

This year was no different.

What *was* different was that this was Matt's first trip as a Windjammer Outing Club junior member.

Stacy had made four or five trips. So Matt had kind of known what to expect. But each year's adventure was unique, too. Mr. and Mrs. Zito, the Outing Club advisors, made sure of that.

Starting in late March right after semester break, the club had met once a week to plan. For months they had pored over road maps and topo maps choosing the route to take, studying the terrain of the site.

Their campsite was somewhere in a huge area in Maine's North Woods identified on maps as Town 7, Range 10.

But there wasn't a town. This unorganized territory was a perfect mix of mountains — not too high — and lakes and streams.

At least that was what Marcie, one of the club members, had said at the last meeting.

Wicked remote, with campsites that could hold the entire group — which this year totaled twelve, plus the Zitos and Wilderness-EMT Jim Morris, the English teacher who also ran as a paramedic with Puckerbrush Rescue.

Gee, Matt thought to himself as he split a blade of grass with his nail, *this is unreal. Plan on something, think about it, can't wait to do it. And in a few minutes, it's all a disaster.*

The day before, he was taking an English final. Now he was here in the woods, wondering how he would ever get out.

Matt thought back with a sad smile to the sunshiny beginning of the day, now eleven hours and several hundred miles away. . . .

He had arrived at the school pickup spot fifteen minutes early, just in case.

The club had rented a van to carry the happy campers and their gear.

When he and Todd and the other guys had been throwing packs up onto the top storage rack of the van, he'd laughed at Marcie's T-shirt:

Support
Search and Rescue
— get lost!

Funny how things turn around and bite you sometimes.

Mrs. Zito had driven. Up the Maine Turnpike, due north.

Through Bangor and Old Town, going alongside the Penobscot River till the Piscataquis River joins it at Howland.

Then the van veered west, followed the Piscataquis to the town of Milo, where they'd turned north again. Passing through both Brownvilles, and on to a logging road.

They'd got to Kathadin Iron Works, then stopped at the gate house for the St. Regis Paper Company's forest preserve.

Mr. Zito signed in with the gatekeeper and paid a toll.

Their campsite was a few miles beyond.

* * *

Matt threw away the grass pieces, swatted a black fly.

Then he sat and scratched. And sat some more — thinking how Todd had warned him about the black flies, right after lunch at their campsite along White Brook. Not so bad now, Todd'd told him, but wait till

99

they know we're here. You have to carry rocks in your pockets just to keep from being carried off.

I bet, Matt said to himself, *Todd has no idea how bad. Here I am, my bug dope used up. I'm the main course at a black fly banquet.*

His stomach felt empty. Nervous. He felt a shiver come over his whole body.

Whoa, Matt told himself. *Get a grip. Got to keep on track, work through this whole day, figure out what happened to get me here.*

Then make a plan.

Think about Todd. Like why did he have to choose me to kid?

Like about the billdads.

Matt wouldn't be in this fix if it weren't for the billdads.

He had been on enough phony snipe hunts to not buy the story about a forest animal called a billdad. It was, he was told, a smallish animal, about ankle high, somewhat like a beaver. It feeds, Marcie had joined in, by stunning trout with a tail-swat which made a *wazzat* sound. *Wazzat!*

What baloney.

Matt had seen Mrs. Zito turn her head to hide a smile.

Why did he agree to go when Todd said there was an excellent billdad stream a half hour away?

Why not?

He thought back. . . .

* * *

He and Todd had been out there looking for fictitious billdads for . . . how long?

Matt checked Todd's watch. Over an hour.

He looked up. The sun disappeared behind dark clouds from the west. A weather system was rolling in.

"Wazzat?" Todd's arm reached back and clamped a hold on Matt. "Didja hear that?"

Dumb. "Naw, I didn't hear a thing." In fact, Matt thought the woods were so quiet it was spooky.

Todd took off. Matt followed, his Merrells lifting a spray of leaves and needles. Todd's boots were the size of meat loaf pans. He seemed to put a foot down every five yards or so.

Matt wished he were that big.

"Hey." Matt pointed. "That storm looks heavy duty. Think we should head back, Todd?"

Matt'd had enough.

"We already are," Todd snapped as he trudged along.

Once or twice Matt paused. It'd been creeping up on him, a foreboding. Where exactly were they off to? But Todd must know, must be keeping track. After all, he was in high school. Right? President of the Outing Club. Right?

That was Matt's first mistake.

Something's wrong here, Matt thought, shaking his head. He didn't know which way to go, but was

101

sure the direction Todd was taking was wrong.

He was positive.

"Look, Todd. You were confused yourself a minute ago. And now you're sure?

"I'm not sure of much, but I *know* I haven't seen that blowdown over there." Matt nodded toward up-rooted spruces, crisscrossed. "We couldn't have come this way."

"So I was turned around," Todd said as he pushed out his chest and tucked in the back of his shirt. "I'm not now. You're acting like we're lost."

Todd made a scoffing noise.

Give me a break, Matt thought, picking at his braces.

Todd's face was close to Matt's. "What're you suggesting, that we go some other way?"

He was in a snit.

Matt looked through the dense damp air for a funnel of smoke from a camp fire.

Anything.

"No," Matt said. "I think we should find a clearing, while we've got time. 'Find a space. And show your face.' That's what we're supposed to do."

Get it together, Todd, Matt thought. But didn't say.

"Hoooo, man," Todd laughed. "Supposed to do *when?* Hey, you want to sit here — fine. Fine. I'll start back, and when I see something familiar, I'll come back and get you."

Matt was silent. He knew this was a bad move. He

also knew nothing he said would change Todd's mind. It had slammed shut like a bear trap.

Todd looked at him, challenged him.

And took off. . . .

* * *

That was, now, over two hours ago.

Todd for some reason must have gone all the way back to camp.

Matt closed his book, *Julie of the Wolves*, and thought for a minute about Julie's struggle in the wilderness.

Hey, if she could survive alone in the Arctic. . . .

He sat up straighter. Thought about himself.

Matt had finished off the last gulp from his water bottle. Now he refilled it at the stream.

He found a grassy knoll in the clearing and lay down. He rolled over, investigated a rotting tree trunk, and watched a colony of ants weave in and out.

He was having trouble figuring out what to do.

Or even concentrating on anything for more than ten seconds.

There he was, fummydiddling around, jumping at every sound, sure that Mr. Zito and the guys were about to pop out from behind a tree.

But what if Todd didn't tell them; if Mr. Zito doesn't know I'm missing.

When he finds out, he'll really be tee'd off.

Matt figured they'd miss him at some point.

Todd was supposed to come back and get him. Maybe Todd's playing games. *It's not a game. It's not a game!*

Or maybe they figure I'm playing around.

"We have here," he said aloud, "what my cousin Davey would call a situation."

He smiled in spite of his fear. Talking to the woods.

Whoa. Is that the first sign of panic? He knew about hunters' syndrome, where they lost their heads, started tearing off clothing, hiding from their rescuers.

No, he decided, *I'm not losing it. It's OK to talk out loud to myself.*

He said his next thought aloud. "It's a good way to judge how I'm doin'." His voice sounded even, smooth.

"I am lost." There. He said it. Not turned around, overdue. "I am lost." No more back and forth on it. A fact.

"Now, since I'm lost . . . what?"

In a way it was a relief.

He knew he needed a plan. He needed to act.

Before darkness set in.

But what was it that Mr. Zito had said last fall? Ninety percent of all overdue persons are found within the first twenty-four hours.

So it was silly to do this planning. Matt would be back in the camp in a few hours, before dark.

They'll find me, he thought.

Then he remembered Mr. Zito telling them that most folks who die in the woods have unused matches and a full thermos.

Just like me.

It was hard enough for him to admit he was lost. It was worse to know he might not be found right away and would have to plan for the long haul.

"I'm planning to be out here all night. Maybe longer." Good. He said it. "I've got to be prepared."

* * *

Inventory. Like Julie did, in my book. To see what I've got to work with.

Matt emptied his pockets and his Puckerbrush Rescue fanny pack.

His face cracked into a smile. Just what I need, he thought as he took out the last three items, a pocket mask and two baseball cards.

He shoved Koufax and Clemens into his shirt and eyed the rest of the pile. All sorts of possibilities; he was amazed.

He picked up his whistle. *I'll blow this three times every half hour until I'm rescued*, he decided.

He blew. Loud and long.

Noise felt good.

The silence, after the noise stopped, was larger than before.

He put his matches, their working ends water-proofed with nail polish, back in their Band-Aid tin. He could get a fire going. If it got bad enough, maybe he'd think about using a baseball card as a starter.

Whodoya burn first?

He didn't think he wanted to burn his book. He might have time to reread it. About thirty times.

Maybe I could burn just the boring pages.

Matt set to work loading his arms with firewood. He decided to gather enough to fill a bathtub — that'd get him through the night.

As his body worked, his mind joined in. He stacked the dry logs in a wall jutting out from the hole left by a lightning-struck oak.

Then he filled its root-hole with evergreen boughs to make a bed.

He'd build his fire in the protected angle between his woodpile and bed.

He scratched at his bites, then bloused the bottom of his pants into his boots. Tucking them in like that would keep the bugs off his legs.

He rolled down his sleeves under his windbreaker.

"A s'more would look great oozing into my camp fire," he said aloud. "I'm hungry."

But face it, there are things I won't be able to do anything about.

Food for example.

His fingers twisted the hem of his windbreaker into a little turban around his finger.

His stomach did that rumble that Chancealong, his chinook pup, made sometimes.

In their survival talk last Tuesday, Jim Morris had

said a kid could stay alive for ten days without food and water if he sat still.

Zero exercise.

He made a decision to move only when he had to. He looked at his hands, and stopped his fiddling.

He popped the gray cap off a black film container, and pinched a mound of kerosene and sawdust mix.

Then he piled kindling over the fire starter.

Fire, shelter, water. Whistle. Find space, show face.

Matt had covered his bases.

I may only be allowed one screw-up, he said to himself as he struck a match. He didn't think he had made it yet.

The fire roared.

* * *

As dusk fell, Matt's mood darkened and his pulse quickened.

Even with the fire, he was cold. Was shivering anyway.

He slapped a black fly. Why weren't *they* chilled?

The shadows were deeper.

He wondered what everyone back at the camp was thinking. Gearing up to come out and search for him maybe?

He hoped.

Then it hit him. He bet they were sitting around trying to figure out what *he* was thinking!

What would Matt do, they were all wondering, if he got lost in the woods? Run around in circles? Climb up the mountain? Follow a river?

Looking for any clues about his behavior.

That made him feel good. Everyone knew that Matt was a levelheaded guy. Mr. Zito would say that Matt would do exactly what he was supposed to do.

Find a space and show your face.

Count on it.

But his face wasn't going to be visible for much more of this day. The blackness was closing in around him.

His courage shrank, a new feeling for him.

He listened to the racket of the night animals.

Matt began to imagine all sorts of horrors. You couldn't pay him a million bucks to run outside his circle of light.

He threw two more logs on the fire.

He started to whimper. "I want to be warm," he mumbled to himself.

"I want to be home. I want OUT."

Afraid, lost, nowhere to hide. "I have no idea where I am."

He whispered to himself so the animals wouldn't hear.

But that wasn't really so. "In a way I'm not lost. I've forgotten how to get somewhere — I've misplaced the camp, that's all."

He wiped his cheeks. *But I know where I am.*

Right here. With these trees. In the North Woods.

So what was he scared of?

For right now, this is my home.

If the birds and the moose can survive here, I can too.

Matt had a bed, some light, some warmth, no bug dope, but plenty of water. Food? He'd have to find some. . . . Be a human animal or an animal human.

Tomorrow he'd watch what the animals do.

Which, he realized as he banked his fire for the night, is what his book's heroine, Julie, did with the Alaskan wolves. She made wolf noises, crawled around on all fours.

He'd do it, too . . . if he had to.

As Matt lay down, the cold air crept into every part of his body.

Hey. Animals don't have blankets.

He curled up, pulling pine branches over him.

Twice during the night he got up to feed his fire. Both times, he blew his whistle. *Tweeeet tweet! Tweeet!*

Matt was a wicked sound sleeper. But he couldn't have slept through the noise that woke him that night. Like black bears crashing through dry cattails.

It scared him. Until he remembered Luke Chapel's story — the lost rock climber that the Wilderness Rescue Team had to tackle to save. The guy was freezing. It was night, and he freaked out at the noise of approaching rescuers.

Took five men to hold him down, according to the paramedic.

Not me, decided Matt. *No way. I'll be cool.*

He wondered if that noise far away was the team coming to save him. . . .

It was the last thought he remembered having. He dozed.

* * *

"Matt . . . Matt . . . MATT!!!!" A hasty team of three trained searchers, sent ahead of other rescuers, was sweeping the area.

Paramedic Jim Morris, Matt's English teacher, was at the lead.

One of them yelled every thirty seconds. That meant that each hasty team member shouted once every minute and a half.

The rhythm set their pace.

"MAAAAT. Ho, MAAAT. Can you hear me?"

Was Matt dreaming?

He opened an eye, couldn't figure out where he was. Then he remembered.

"Here I am! HELLLLPPPP! Hey, I'm heeeeeere! Me, Matt!"

The black bears-in-cattails noises stopped.

"Matt?" asked a voice tentatively.

"I'm here. Here. Over here. It's me. Matt."

Then they were there with him, their headlamps playing all over him. "Howya doin', Matt?" Asking how he felt, if he was hurt.

110

Someone placed a down jacket over his shoulders.

He felt perfect. Great. Like crawling under the covers on a cold winter evening and pulling them up over your head. Relaxing your body as the warmth sweeps over.

Matt would never again feel so . . . *found*.

And stupid, of course. He felt dumb.

"I guess," he said, looking down at the insulated coat bundled around his hands, "Todd must be some mad. Not that I blame him."

The jerk, he thought to himself.

"Todd?" Jim Morris straightened. "Where *is* Todd? Not here?"

John held his radio to his mouth: "Portable-9, Search and Rescue Command," he said. "Advise you request permission to upgrade to SAR Level Two. We've located one, but the other kid is still Ten-60 and" — glancing at lowering clouds and fog — "the Ten-13's deteriorating."

*To find out what happens to Todd,
read the next EMERGENCY RESCUE! book*

Nightmare at Norton's Mills

SKILL
Find a Space/Show Your Face

WHAT is it? Knowing what to do when lost in the wilderness. Counting on yourself when you can't activate the 9-1-1 system.

WHY do you do it? To help searchers locate you, and to survive until they do.

WHEN do you do it? While you have daylight. Sit right down and study your surroundings. Do you hear or see anything — smoke, a truck, a chain saw — to lead you out of your dilemma? If you are lost, face it. Stop thinking about how to find your way back. Instead use your energy to plan, like Matt did. Todd never accepted that he was lost, and he's still out there.

HOW do you do it? 1) Find an open place where you can be spotted from the ground or from the air. Choose a location with water, firewood, and natural shelter. 2) Find or construct a place to sleep. 3) Gather a bathtubful of wood to feed your fire overnight. 4) Enjoy your fire's light and heat. Dry your clothes. Your fire will make you feel better. It will also act as a signal for searchers. 5) Don't be afraid of rescuers, who'll look and sound scary at night. Don't worry that people will be mad at you for getting lost;

they'll be thrilled to see you. 6) Wait. For as long as it takes. Someone will be along to pick you up. Be patient. 7) Panic is your greatest enemy. Don't lose your best survival tool — your head.

Is the scene safe?

When you are lost and alone, only your own good sense can make the scene safe.

* * *

To learn more about safety in the woods, read *Take a Hike! The Sierra Club Kids' Guide to Hiking and Backpacking*, by Lynne Foster, published by Little, Brown and Company, Inc., 1991.

Emergency Rescue! Report

Report number	5	My name	MATT RICH

Incident location IN THE
TOWN 7, RANGE 10 — WOODS
street
UNORGANIZED
TERRITORY   MAINE
city/town   state

My address
BAY VIEW STREET
street
CAMDEN, ME. 04843
city/town   state   zip

Was the scene safe? yes no
Describe the scene. ☒ ☐

I GOT TURNED AROUND IN THE
NORTH WOODS

First name of victim	Age	male	female	Aid first given by
ME	14	☒	☐	☐ me ☒ someone else ☐ EMTs ☐ police SAR ☐ firefighters

Transported to   BACK TO CAMP

Describe any transportation
or communication problems.   NONE, ONCE
THEY FOUND ~~ME~~ ARRIVED!

Type of illness or injury or accident

- ☐ bone fracture
- ☐ aches and sprains
- ☐ bleeding injury
- ☐ illness
- ☐ fire
- ☐ auto or truck accident
- ☐ water incident
- ☐ HazMat
- ☐ airplane disaster
- ☒ lost person/search and rescue
- ☐ extrication
- ☐ animal incident
- ☐ electrical accident
- ☐ tornado
- ☐ hurricane
- ☐ blizzard
- ☐ other

Who called for help?

- ☒ me ? BLEW A WHISTLE
- ☐ a friend MR. ZITO REALIZED
- ☐ family member TODD AND I WERE
- ☐ professional MISSING AT DINNER
  responder AND ALERTED THE
- ☐ neighbor
- ☐ other person MAINE WARDEN SERVICE

Emergency responders on the scene

- ☐ EMTs
- ☐ firefighters
- ☐ police
- ☐ HazMat
- ☐ emergency department
- ☐ utility crew
- ☒ search and rescue

Describe what happened, and the outcome. Include unusual
circumstances. TODD THOUGHT HE COULD FIND HIS WAY BACK, BUT
I WASN'T SURE. SO I FOUND A SPACE AND SHOWED MY FACE.
I ALSO MADE A SHELTER AND BUILT A FIRE. I WAS
PRETTY HAPPY WHEN MR. MORRIS FOUND ME IN THE
MIDDLE OF THE NIGHT. BUT WE STILL DON'T KNOW
WHAT HAPPENED TO TODD.
my signature Matt Rich

Emergency Rescue!
Vocabulary

access: an opening made by emergency responders, such as cutting a roof off a wrecked car, to remove a victim

adrenaline: this chemical, made by the body and released when you get excited, also reverses allergic reactions

allergy: a sensitivity to things like certain foods, medicines, dust, venom, pollen

anaphylaxis: an allergic over-reaction that can cause death

arteries: oxygen-rich blood flows away from the heart through these hollow tubes

backboard: an injured person is strapped to this long flat device so his or her spine won't move

beeper: a radio receiver, the size of a stack of base-ball cards, that lets rescuers know when they are needed

blood pressure: the force of the pumping heart as it squeezes blood throughout the body

blood pressure cuff: a cloth-covered rubber sleeve pumped tight around the upper arm to stop blood-flow, then loosened until a stethoscope hears blood moving again

bunker pants: heavy fireproof/waterproof trousers

carotid: blood fresh with oxygen flows through this artery from the heart to the brain

CB: citizen band: a two-way radio used by civilians, like truckers, to talk to one another while on the road

certification: training and testing for emergency responders

CHEMTREC: a telephone ꞁot line for chemical emergencies, paid for by the chemicals industry

CHLOREP: an acronym for Chlorine Emergency Planning, these teams offer professional help when a HazMat incident involves chlorine

claustrophobia: a fear of small, confining places

cocoon: a head-to-toes sealed protective unit worn by HazMat responders

copy: in radio language, to receive and understand the message

cyanosis: a bluish, purple skin color caused by too little oxygen in the blood

diabetic: a person whose body has trouble moving sugar from the bloodstream into other spaces

disorientation: confusion identified when someone can't remember his name, his location, or the day

dispatch: slang for dispatcher who answers emergency calls, sends responders, then coaches callers until help is on the scene

dyspnea: difficult or labored breathing caused by injury or illness

EMS: Emergency Medical Services: the network of medical responders — from citizen responders like you, to dispatchers, EMTs, and finally, hospital emergency department doctors and nurses

EMT: emergency medical technician: a responder who treats patients at the scene and in the ambulance on the way to the hospital

epinephrine: nicknamed epi and another name for adrenaline, this chemical turns around allergic reactions

ETA: radio-talk for estimated time of arrival; when an ambulance, for example, will arrive

extrication: getting people out of plane wrecks, stuck elevators, and other emergency situations after access is made

femur: the thigh bone, the largest in the body

fibula: leg bone from the knee to the ankle, right behind the tibia

first responder: the emergency rescuer first at the scene

flammable: catches fire easily

flush: flowing oxygen to a victim at the highest setting

hasty team: the first-responding search and rescue team: a few trained joggers who look quickly in the most likely areas for an overdue person

HazMat: any hazardous material which in small quantities causes damage to people, animals, or the environment

histamine: when the body senses an enemy invader, this slippery chemical tries to flood out the bad guys by causing hives, runny eyes, and dripping noses

hives: water-filled cells that form itchy body-bumps

hunters' syndrome: irrational behavior that lowers the possibility of rescue and survival for lost people

immediate isolation distance: the minimum safe distance from a HazMat spill

injector: a tube, with a needle on one end and a plunger on the other, for shooting medicine through the skin

IV: in Latin, *intra venous* means within the vein: IV fluids and medicines drip down from a bag, through a hollow needle stuck into the back of the hand, and end up in the bloodstream

MedicAlert: a bracelet or necklace alerting rescuers to a life-threatening medical problem

MOI: mechanism of injury: how a victim was injured

monitor: also called an EKG or ECG, EMTs learn from this machine how well the heart is working

packaging: EMT-slang for splinting, bandaging, long-boarding, and/or strapping a patient onto a stretcher for transport to the hospital

paralysis: inability to feel and move a portion of the body

paramedic: a person with the highest EMT certification

patella: the rounded bone at the front of the knee; the knee cap

placard: a diamond-shaped sign identifying the hazardous material — HazMat — on board

pocket mask: this small plastic rescue-breathing device protects the rescuer from the victim's germs

portable: short for **portable** radio, and also used to identify a rescuer through his portable number; for example, David Mountain, Sr., is **Portable**-68, and Jill Mountain is **Portable**-40

psychogenic reaction: nervousness or excitement that causes the patient to faint

pulmonary edema: fluid-filled swollen lungs that make breathing difficult or impossible

pulse: this beat of the pumping heart can be felt wherever an artery stretches over a bone — at the wrist, on the top of the feet, along the neck

quick-hitches: another name for bunker pants, these firefighter pants pull up quickly

radial pulse: the heartbeat felt inside the wrist, up on the thumb side

remote: more than one hour away from a hospital

rescue breathing: using the rescuer's breath to deliver oxygen to a person who is not breathing

resuscitate: to revive

rig: nickname for an ambulance

Ringer's solution: used in an IV setup to add fluids to the body

rock 'n' roll: to package and transport to a hospital as quickly as possible

run: an emergency response, starting when rescuers are called and ending when they and their rig are back in the station

safe zone: in a HazMat incident, the area beyond danger

SAR: search and rescue: an organized attempt to find an overdue person

scanner: this radio receiver loops through pre-set emergency frequencies, and stops whenever it picks up conversation or a tone

SCBA: self-contained breathing apparatus; firefighters and HazMat teams use these air tanks and masks in unbreathable environments

sharps box: a container for throwing away used medical needles and other skin-penetrating objects

shock: this dire emergency results when blood

stops delivering oxygen throughout the body

sniffing position: the angle to hold a head when opening an airway, as if the victim were smelling the wind

stat: immediately; hustle!

stethoscope: EMTs use this instrument to listen to heart and lung sounds

suction: to vacuum vomit, blood, and froth from a victim's mouth or throat

terrain: the rise and fall of the land

tib-fib: the two bones, tibia and fibula, sistered together in the lower leg

tibia: the shin bone, right in front of the fibula

topo(graphy) map: chart used to understand the lay of the land — mountains, plains, hills, valleys

toxic: poisonous

traffic: in rescue language, conversation on a radio or scanner

transport: to take a victim from the scene to the hospital's emergency department

trauma: an injury or wound

turnout gear: the waterproof/fireproof clothing and equipment a firefighter wears at an emergency scene

vein: a hollow tube carrying blood back to the heart

warden: a Maine forest ranger

wilderness-EMT: an emergency medical technician

specially trained to give care to patients far from ambulance and hospital

woofer: a wilderness first responder who has first-aid training and deals with emergencies in remote environments

About the Authors

JAMES and LOIS COWAN don't just write about emergency situations — they live them. As professional volunteer fire, medical, and search responders, they run with Maine's Wilderness Rescue Team and Atlantic Engine Company #2, and belong to the National Association of Search and Rescue, the National Association of EMS Physicians, and the National Writers Union. The EMT trainers and Red Cross CPR instructors teach emergency skills to police officers, Alaskan guides, and schoolchildren. They also write newspaper columns and lecture on survival strategies.

When not rescuing or writing, the Cowans toboggan race and double-row their peapod boat on Penobscot Bay. They have eight children from 34 to 12, and live in a converted church in Camden, Maine.

Look for
the next Emergency Rescue! book:
Nightmare at Norton's Mills
by James and Lois Cowan

Todd was a basket case.

It was now a day and a half that he'd been lost.

His clothes were torn and dirty. His knees were scraped. Face, neck, and forearm were covered with welts, scratched raw.

Todd felt hungry, frightened, and abandoned.

His shouted conversation with a non-existent Matt — "You can't fool me, Matt!" — was crazed. "I know you're right behind that tree. Stop hiding!"

For the first six hours after he had left Matt, Todd had a plan. He'd aimed to get to the top of a ridge where he could look out and find something familiar. Then run back and get Matt, as he had promised.

But every ridge he climbed seemed to lead higher.

There was always in the distance another spot, offering a better view.

His spirits sank with dusk. Fog didn't help.

Losing his sight had always been Todd's greatest fear. He never played games like Blind Man's Bluff or Marco Polo. Now he was trapped within the pitch-black darkness of the Maine woods.

When the rain rolled in from the west at dawn the next morning, Todd was caught unprepared.

Since then, he had walked in cold, wet clothes.

"I see you, Matt. Hah!" he yelled at a shadow deep in the gloom.

Todd was physically and emotionally whipped.

As the evening of the second day rolled around, once again the weather was going down the tubes.

Todd wasn't far behind.

*Share your emergency adventures
with the authors!*

Whenever you witness an emergency, send us your filled-out Emergency Rescue! Report, on the next page. Even if you don't have an incident to report right now, we'd still love to know what you like about our *EMERGENCY RESCUE!* books. We will respond to your letter or report. Ten-04?

The Cowans
EMERGENCY RESCUE!
Mountain Street
Camden, ME 04843

Emergency Rescue! Report Instructions

1. If this book is borrowed from a library or a friend, you need to make a copy of the Emergency Rescue! Report form, on the opposite page. If this is your own book, tear or cut out the page.
2. Fill out the Emergency Rescue! Report form.
3. Then fold on the dotted line.
4. Tape or staple the unfolded bottom edges shut.
5. Place a stamp where it says to.
6. Mail it.

Emergency Rescue! Report

| Report number | My name |
| Incident location | My address |

street | street

city/town   state | city/town   state   zip

Was the scene safe?   yes   no
Describe the scene.   ☐   ☐

| First name of victim   Age   male   female | Aid first given by |

male ☐   female ☐

Transported to

Aid first given by
☐ me
☐ someone else
☐ EMTs
☐ police
☐ firefighters

Describe any transportation
communication problems.

Type of illness or injury or accident

bone fracture
aches and sprains
bleeding injury
illness
fire
auto or truck accident
water incident
HazMat
airplane disaster
lost person/search and rescue
extrication
animal incident
electrical accident
tornado
hurricane
blizzard
other

Who called for help?

☐ me
☐ a friend
☐ family member
☐ professional
     responder
☐ neighbor
☐ other person

Emergency responders on the scene

☐ EMTs
☐ firefighters
☐ police
☐ HazMat
☐ emergency department
☐ utility crew
☐ search and rescue

Describe what happened, and the outcome. Include unusual
circumstances.

my signature _____

Staple or tape shut . . . stamp . . . and mail.

Plac
star
here

Emergency Rescue!
Mountain Street
Camden, Maine 04843